LARGE PRINT   10/9/14 $35.95
F   978-1-62899-234-2
BER
Bertino, Marie-Helene
2 A.M. at The Cat's Pajamas

2 A.M.
at The Cat's
Pajamas

Center Point
Large Print

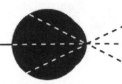

**This Large Print Book carries the
Seal of Approval of N.A.V.H.**

2 A.M. at The Cat's Pajamas

Marie-Helene Bertino

CENTER POINT LARGE PRINT
THORNDIKE, MAINE

This Center Point Large Print edition is published in the year 2014 by arrangement with Crown Publishers, an imprint of the Crown Publishing Group, a division of Random House LLC, New York.

Grateful acknowledgment is made to Blossom Dearie Music for permission to reprint an excerpt from "Blossom's Blues," copyright © 1956 by Blossom Dearie Music. All Rights Reserved. Reprinted by permission of Blossom Dearie Music, as administered by Jim DiGionvanni.

The text of this Large Print edition is unabridged. In other aspects, this book may vary from the original edition.
Printed in the United States of America on permanent paper.
Set in 16-point Times New Roman type.

ISBN: 978-1-62899-234-2

Library of Congress Cataloging-in-Publication Data

Bertino, Marie-Helene.
2 a.m. at The Cat's Pajamas / Marie-Helene Bertino. — Center Point Large Print edition.
pages ; cm
Summary: "As three lost souls search for love, music and hope on the snow-covered streets of Philadelphia, together they will discover life's endless possibilities over the course of one magical night"—Provided by publisher.
ISBN 978-1-62899-234-2 (library binding : alk. paper)
1. Large type books. I. Title. II. Title: Two a.m. at The Cat's Pajamas.
PS3602.E7683A613 2014b
813'.6—dc23
2014025773

Mom,
You said, *some people invest in prizefighters, I'll invest in you.* It was one of those gray nights when (everyone took the easy way out) I did not feel strong. This book is for you (Helene Bertino), for turning me into a prizefighter, with grace.

"Yes, [Philadelphia is] horrible, but in a very interesting way. There were places there that had been allowed to decay, where there was so much fear and crime that just for a moment there was an opening to another world."

—DAVID LYNCH

2 A.M. at The Cat's Pajamas

*I*t is dark, dark seven A.M. on Christmas Eve Eve.

Snow flurries fall in the city. Actors walking home from a cast party on Broad Street try to catch them on their tongues. The ingénue lands a flake on her hot cheek and erupts into a fit of laughter. In Fishtown a nightmare trembles through the nose and paws of a dog snoozing under construction flats. The Rittenhouse Square fountain switches to life with a pronouncement of water while Curtis Hall musicians, late for final rehearsal, arpeggiate through the park.

The flurries somersault, reconsider, double back. The Ninth Street alleys bear witness as they softly change their minds. Mrs. Rose Santiago, shawl knotted beneath her chin, uses a broom to convince them away from her stoop. They refuse to land. She sweeps uselessly at the air.

In her room at the prow of her father's apartment, Madeleine Altimari practices the shimmy. Shoulders, shoulders, shoulders. In front of the mirror, so she can judge herself, face sharp with focus. It is the world's most serious shimmy. After thirty seconds, a flamingo-shaped timer trills and hops on its plastic legs. Madeleine stops shimmying and rejoins a Menthol 100 dozing in an ashtray on her vanity.

She exhales. "Again."

On the record player, Blossom Dearie says she's alive, she's awake, she's aware. Shoulders, shoulders, shoulders. After thirty seconds, the timer trills again.

Madeleine frowns at herself in the mirror. "Terrible." On a list by the ashtray, she marks *one minute* next to *The Shimmy,* followed by a pert *C minus*. She drags on the cigarette. The other categories—*Singing, Scales, Guitar*—are unmarked.

Madeleine is two days away from being ten.

She wears a clothespin on her nose and the uniform for Saint Anthony of the Immaculate Heart: a maroon sweater over a gray jumper over a gold shirt over a training bra with lemon-colored stitching. Thick, maroon tights. She is number three in fifth-grade height-ordered lineups, behind Maisie, whose spine is shaped like a question mark, and Susan, the daughter of ballerinas. She read somewhere a clothespin worn religiously will shrink her unignorable nose. She thinks the occasional glimmers she can see through her window are snow flurries. She has trouble spelling the word *rhythm*. She likes when people in movies go to see movies. She cannot understand why the dime is worth more than the fatter, wider nickel. She needs a haircut. Her favorite singer is Blossom Dearie and her favorite bass is upright. She spent the previous night dreaming of apples. She smokes Newport Menthols from the carton her mother was smoking when she died the previous year.

Eggs cuss and snap on the kitchen stove.

The unofficial rule of Saint Anthony of the Immaculate Heart is that Madeleine is never allowed to sing again in church or at any assembly. Never, never, a whole page of nevers. Even though she had nothing to do with what happened at the previous year's Winter Assembly. Still, it is going to be a gold star day. She will suffer through Clare Kelly's singing in morning mass, the girl's nasal notes and plosive p's filling the church with godless noise, spritzing the first row of pews with every heretical t, BUT THEN, her class will be making caramel apples. Madeleine has never had a caramel apple and she wants to taste one more than she wants God's love.

Clare, the sound Madeleine's toilet makes when it's dry. Madeleine is forever adding water to its basin when it wails, from the purpose-specific can she keeps under the sink.

Like a comet, a horrific afterthought, a roach darts down the wall. Its path follows indecipherable logic. Madeleine screams in high C and crushes the cigarette. She pivots, rips a paper towel from a roll on her nightstand. The roach halts, teasing coordinates out of the air with its antennae. It senses her and is rendered paralyzed by options. Madeleine closes her eyes, makes the sound of a train whistle on a prairie, and squeezes. Ninth Street Market roaches are full and round like tomatoes. This one leaves a mark on the wall but most of it gets flushed down the toilet. She scrubs her hands. Breathes in and out. Every day, more and more roaches. Every time she kills one, Madeleine worries she is a bad person. *Stop worrying,* she instructs herself. *It's time to sing.*

She changes the record and releases the clothespin from her nose. She locks eyes with herself in the mirror and waits for the music to start.

Madeleine sings.

My name is Blossom
I was raised in a lion's den.

One hand is perched on her hip while the other swings back and forth, keeping time. Tucked into the mirror of her vanity, a picture of her mother singing: one hand on her hip, the other swinging back and forth, in time. Her mother was a dancer and singer whose voice could redirect the mood of a room.

My nightly occupation
Is stealing other women's men.

After the cancer spread to her lymph nodes, Madeleine's mother filled a recipe box with instructions on how to do various things she knew

she wouldn't be around to teach her. HOW TO
MAKE A FIST, HOW TO CHANGE A FLAT, HOW TO
WRITE A THANK-YOU NOTE FOR A GIFT YOU
HATE, HOW TO BE EFFICIENT: *Whenever you
are doing one thing, ask yourself: what else could
I be doing?* On one recipe card, Madeleine's
mother listed the rules of singing.

The #1 rule: KNOW YOURSELF.

Madeleine knows she frowns in the silence
between lines. She knows if she straightens her
spine she can hit more notes than if she hunches.
She knows she makes up in full-throatedness what
she lacks in technical ability. She knows how to
harmonize, with anything, with someone talking,
that harmony is what melody carries in its pocket.
She can burrow into a line of music and search out
unexpected melodies. She can scat. She knows
she scats better if she has eaten a light breakfast.
She knows an empty orb hovers inside her, near
where the ovaries are drawn on the foldout in her
health textbook: the diaphragm. In the diaphragm,
the weather is always seventy degrees and sunny.
Unable to be shaken even when she shakes.
Madeleine has trained herself to, when she falters
on a high note, clasp the reins of her diaphragm
and gather.

The song is over. In her flamingo notebook,
Madeleine marks *Blossom's Blues* next to *Singing*.
The scatting was flat but had soul. *B minus,* she
writes.

The eggs are ready. She slides them onto a plate and adds a square of toast and a spoonful of jam. She holds her breath as she steps into her father's bedroom. He is sleeping, his back toward her. She clears medicine bottles, an ashtray, a half-empty glass of water, to make space for the plate on his dresser.

Normally she leaves his breakfast and skedaddles, however this morning she wants to feel close to something. She places her hand on his arm. It moves up and down in sleep. Madeleine breathes in and out, in time.

"Eggs," she whispers.

In her bedroom, she peers through the curtains to confirm that the glimmers are flurries. Using mittens, boots, a scarf, and an umbrella, Madeleine turns herself into a warm, dry house.

7:10 A.M.

*I*n the back bedroom of the Kelly family's row home, Clare Kelly plaits her second, perfect braid. She administers advice to her little sister who sits on the bed, transfixed. Clare is proud of herself for allowing Elissa to pal around. She can learn from Clare's mistakes—not that there have been many—and her achievements—which have been plentiful, praise God. Student of the Week, Month, and Year certificates pose on her wall.

Clare finishes the braid with a pink barrette and admires herself. The barrettes will reflect the light of Saint Anthony's stained glass when Father Gary announces, "Clare Kelly will now lead us in the responsorial song." She will step-touch to the foot of the altar under the worshipful gazes of her classmates. Step-touch to genuflect at the statue of Mary, making full stops on her forehead, breastplate, left collarbone, right collarbone. Step-touch to the microphone.

Clare Kelly never has shark fins when she combs her hair into a ponytail, and her braids always part diplomatically.

Her mother gazes at her daughters from the doorway. "Time to go to school."

Clare is proud of herself for being the kind of daughter who doesn't rebel against her parents.

17

Even when they told her she was having a little sister after they'd promised she'd be an only child. She could have answered "garbage" when they pointed to her mother's swollen belly and asked what she thought was in there. But did she say garbage, or a stocking of poop or a lizard? No. Clare Kelly said, "My li'l sister," taking care to furbish "little" with an adorable slur.

Clare helps Elissa into her backpack before donning her own. The Kelly girls file down the carpeted stairs, past the makeshift bar with a sign that reads *Kelly's Pub*, to where their father waits, cheek thrust out in anticipation of each girl's kiss. Every day this kiss, then the short city walk to school. Clare, then Elissa plants one on Dad's smooth cheek and Mom opens the door. Flurries fall in the halo of streetlights. Clare elbows Elissa out of the way. She wants to be first into this snow-wonderful world.

It is her last conscious thought before being struck by a speeding bicyclist.

Clare is hurled against the brightening sky by the force of the handlebars against her thigh. The rider, sliding on his side, meets her falling figure against the base of an electric pole. As if they planned.

Elissa's screaming hits enviable notes. What range that little girl has!

7:15 A.M.

*C*afé Santiago comprises the bottom level of a two-story, aggressively flower-boxed building on Ninth Street. The store fits a table with eight chairs and three display cases selling sweets and prepared foods that vary daily depending on Mrs. Santiago's moods. Christmas cacti bloom in empty gravy cans on the windowsills. Above the counter hangs a life-sized portrait of Mrs. Santiago's late husband, Daniel. Mrs. Santiago lives on the second floor with her dog, Pedro, who is currently, on Christmas Eve Eve, missing.

She stands behind the counter feeding sausage mixture into a casing machine, coaxing out smooth links from the other side. The shop smells like fennel, the cold, and coffee.

Sarina Greene, fifth-grade art teacher at Saint Anthony of the Immaculate Heart, peers into a display case, weighing the merits of three different kinds of caramel. She sways to the instrumental jazz playing on the café's speakers and points to a pile of stately cubes. "Would you say this caramel is sweet or more chalky?"

"Sweet," says Mrs. Santiago.

"That would be good for Brianna but not for the other Brianna," Sarina says.

"How many do you need?"

"Only one, I suppose, but it's a popular name. We call one Brie to keep them straight."

"How many," Mrs. Santiago says, "kinds of caramel?"

Sarina grimaces. "My brain's not working today. I looked for my keys for ten minutes. They were in my hand."

"Must be love."

"Ha!" Sarina cries. Mrs. Santiago's elbow startles a stack of coffee filters. She stoops to collect them. "I don't know how many kinds I need," Sarina says. "I have twenty-four students. Leigh is allergic to everything and Duke is diabetic. He'd turn red if he ate a caramel apple. Become unresponsive and die."

Mrs. Santiago blinks. "We don't want that."

"Which caramel would you use?"

"Medium dark."

"Fine." Sarina nods. It is her first year back in her hometown since high school, summoned by her mother's death and the aching blank page that follows divorce. She counteracts the feeling of being a failure by plunging into every task like a happy doe into brush. Today: these caramels. Last night: spelling each of her student's names in glitter on the brims of twenty-four Santa hats.

"One pound?" Mrs. Santiago says. "A pound and a half?"

Sarina's phone begins its embarrassing call at the bottom of her purse: "Wonderwall." She roots through her bag, finds what she thinks is her phone, and shows it to herself—calculator. She paws through tissues, a sewing kit, her wallet, pipe cleaners, a parking voucher from a crochet class she tried, where she made a tote bag, this tote bag, out of old T-shirts—it is kicky but contains too many caverns. The song continues its assault, then—at last—her phone.

Her grade partner is calling, a woman who finds no situation over which she can't become frantic. Sarina dumps the call into voice mail. The bells of the door clatter. Georgina McGlynn enters from the dark, shaking snowflakes from her coat. Sarina and Georgina, who everyone calls Georgie, went to high school together.

"Picking up a pie for tonight," Georgie says with an apologetic air. As if she needs a reason to be in this shop at this hour. This cues Mrs. Santiago, who disappears into the back.

"Pie is . . ." Sarina says.

The women look in different directions. No radio plays. The street hovers between night and dawn. This is the second time they've run into each other in the neighborhood, both times marked by stammering and adamant friendliness.

"Key lime," says Georgie.

"Wonderful."

"You should come!" Georgie's volume frightens both of them. "It's the old gang."

Sarina has never been part of a gang. "Tonight?"

she says, then remembers Georgie has already said tonight. A forgotten flurry announces itself on the top of her head. It burns wet. "I can't tonight."

"You must." Georgie's tone is panicked. "They would love to see you. Michael, Ben . . ."

Mrs. Santiago returns with the pie.

"You don't want this bag of potatoes hanging around," Sarina says.

The room's silence doubles down. Sarina has no idea why, in the presence of this ex–punk queen from high school, she is compelled to insult herself. Bundling the pie, Mrs. Santiago tsks.

"You're not a bag of potatoes," Georgie says. "Is that 'Wonderwall'?"

Sarina searches the bag again. This time it's Marcos, her ex-husband. "Must be Call Sarina Day," she jokes, dumping the call into voice mail. Georgie wasn't present for the other phone call, she realizes. So the joke makes no sense and Sarina now seems like a girl who rejoices upon receiving any communication from the outside world.

"Key lime." Mrs. Santiago passes it over the counter and Georgie pays. She pulls a card from her wallet and hands it to Sarina.

"Call if you change your mind." She bells onto the street, pie in hand.

Sarina says, "Two pounds."

Mrs. Santiago weighs and bags the caramel.

Is it Sarina's imagination or did Georgie pause

for the length of a sock in the jaw before Ben's name? On the sidewalk outside the shop, a mechanical carousel horse leaps to nowhere. "What's the deal with that horse?" she says.

Mrs. Santiago looks up from the scale, her face still arranged in an expression of scrutiny. "The deal?"

Sarina's grade partner is calling again. She answers.

"Clare Kelly . . . has been attacked by a biker!"

Sarina apologizes to Mrs. Santiago with her eyes, gathers her bags of caramel, and slips outside. Flurries second-guess through the alleys. "Is she dead?"

"She's at the hospital now, poor lamb. I called Principal Randles. We need to find a replacement to sing at this morning's mass. But who? When she sings it's like God is hugging you."

Sarina supports her bags on the carousel horse and rolls her eyes. Her opinion on God: You work your side of the street, I'll work mine. She mentally sorts her students for a singer. The twins, James and Jacob, two variations on the same, dull boy. Brianna, the other Brianna. Maxwell, Devon, Mackenzie. A classroom of girls angling for a future in swimsuit modeling. Maybe don't name your kid on an empty stomach. Her mind's eye rests on Madeleine, a hastily combed little girl in the third row. She recalls some teacher's lounge gossip: Madeleine, assembly, singing.

"What about Madeleine?" she says.

"Good Lord, no," her grade partner chortles. "She sang last year but it was . . . unpleasant. I doubt the principal thinks of that day fondly."

"She was that bad?"

"Did I say she was bad?" the woman says. "Things happened."

"If we need a singer, she's all I have," Sarina says.

"She probably won't want to sing after what happened."

"What happened?"

"It was unpleasant. Let's leave it at that."

Sarina freshens her tone. "I could ask her."

"You could."

"I will." Sarina hangs up.

Mrs. Santiago has waited for her to end the call. The window between them, the women wave good-bye. Sarina mouths the words: *Thank you.*

"My pleasure," Mrs. Santiago says, at full volume.

You can hear through the window, Sarina realizes. Another stunning miscalculation on her part.

7:30 A.M.

In Fishtown, beneath a pile of construction flats, Pedro the dog launches out of a nightmare. The bear that chased him becomes an advertisement pasted to the bottom of a box, a tax attorney with reasonable rates.

Pedro is an open-air pooch, not prone to evenings at home. His joints are nimble and his snout superb. He spent the previous night following the scent of a bitch, pink notes and hydrangea and dung. The pursuit led him out of the meat and coffee smells of his neighborhood to the minty trash of Fishtown. Flirting around the periphery of his brain is an idea both completely vivid and at the same time so malleable that it is not only an image but a hope. When he moves from one street to the next he feels he is moving more toward himself. He is lonely and knows he is lonely. He is in love but is not sure with whom.

As the dog awakens, the city awakens. Crust on its windshields and hungry. Snorting plumes of frustration in the harbor. Scratching its traffic on the expressway. Bone cold and grouchy, from the toes of its stadiums to the strands of its El. One by one each Main Line town revs its city-bound trains. Against the light of dawn, their track lamps are as worthless as rich girls.

Good morning, the city says. *Fuck you.*

The dog does not consider himself lost, though several neighborhoods away, his person's worry manifests in food prep. Fat sausage and sweet bread. The flurried sidewalk dampens his paws as he sniffs around a fire hydrant. Her? Her? A street vent. Her? The trunk of a tree that in warmer months brags cherry blossoms. Her? A stretch of fog-colored siding, then a blunt interruption—the cement steps of the Red Lion Diner.

Inside at the counter, Officer Len Thomas finishes his breakfast. This final bite, the corner of toast dipped in the bit of ketchup piled with the last of the eggs, is the culmination of ten minutes of planning. Napkin dispensers on the counter: gorged, gleaming birds. He chews thirty times, gives up after sixteen, dabs his mouth with the napkin, and with a succinct gesture signals for the check.

The waitress, who had to promise him twice that she understood what *dry* meant, watches a television that hangs in the corner. A famous actress is coming to town. The waitress does not see Len's gesture or hear the whistle he adds when he performs it again. She is officiating the marriage of two bottles of ketchup; overturning one and balancing it on the mouth of the other so it can empty its shit.

The man whistles again. The waitress turns around and in one fluid motion replaces his plate with the check. It strikes Len, still enjoying the slide of egg-bread-ketchup down his throat, that the waitress and the actress have physical traits in common. If the waitress lost twenty pounds and straightened her hair she could be the actress's fatter, less attractive cousin. Len unfolds his wallet and counts out bills. The waitress doesn't hide her interest in the badge and picture in his wallet: a Sears shot of Margaret holding their alarmed-looking son.

"Your wife?" she says.

"Ex." Len flips the wallet shut. "The Cat's Pajamas is on this block, right?"

"Next block." This man has rejected her niceties, so the waitress returns to a glare. "Not open this early, though."

"They'll open for me." Len forces a laugh.

"Sor-ree, Mr. President."

"You look like her." He counts out a tip. "That actress."

"Nah," she says.

"Change?" he reminds her.

She rings him up and deposits the change onto his palm. "Good luck with Lorca."

"Pardon?"

"Cat's Pajamas, right?" She turns her attention back to the television.

Outside, Len unrolls a stick of gum from a pack he keeps in his breast pocket. He's accustomed to people not liking him. The waitress, everyone in

27

the Boston precinct he left behind, and probably whoever this club owner is whose day he's about to ruin. The morning feels scraped clean. He folds the wrapper into a neat square and tosses it into a nearby trash can. He knows the numbers on his license plate add up to fourteen. He knows the latch on his belt is centered because he has checked, twice. A dog sniffing a newspaper stand notices him. Perfect flakes twitch in his whiskers.

"Hello, pooch," Len says.

The dog finds nothing it needs in the figure of Len Thomas and goes back to searching.

8:00 A.M.

*T*he only sojourn Madeleine is permitted to make alone is the half-block walk to Café Santiago every morning to eat her breakfast. It is one of the many rules that snap frames around her newly motherless life. No alleys. No sleepovers. No going anywhere except Santiago's after school.

Her apartment complex is shaped like a horseshoe; her father's apartment is on the fullest swell of the round. In the center stands a half-hearted fountain that has surrendered to time and inattention. Madeleine marches past it, through the arch that leads to the street, past the store of stained-glass lamps (a line of dancers; their jeweled heads bow), through the cobbled alley (screw off, rules), to the blue carousel horse in front of Café Santiago. She rests her mittened hand on the horse's saddle.

"Hello, horse," she whispers.

Madeleine can feel its yearning to go up and down, its hooves frozen in midgallop. Slipping a quarter into its rusted change box would elicit nothing but a lost quarter. It's busted, marooned and affixed to the sidewalk by an indiscreet pole, with no carnival for miles and no equine company. But Madeleine loves the horse, and saying good morning to it is one of her traditions. Skipping it would feel as uncomfortable as an incorrectly buttoned coat.

Inside the shop, Madeleine unlayers her outer garments by the door. Mrs. Santiago fries sausage behind the counter; the café is filled with the pleasant crackling of a vinyl LP. On the table, a stack of chocolate chip pancakes, a cup of black coffee, and the newspaper, opened to the Entertainment section. Madeleine delivers a kiss to Mrs. Santiago's cheek and sits.

Mrs. Santiago is a lumpy woman in a state of continuous fluster. Most of the business of her face is conducted on the top half: forehead, mournful eyes, and tiny nose lined up in short order. Her mouth, dime-sized, is usually arranged in a surprised purse, giving her the effect of a holiday cherub, the light-up kind currently decorating the neighborhood's abbreviated yards.

Mrs. Santiago evaluates all situations through the prism of her late husband Daniel's likes and dislikes. Daniel liked good posture, gingersnaps, and aloe plants. To Mrs. Santiago, a good world is straight posture, gingersnaps, and aloe plants. "Your teacher was just in buying caramel," she says.

Madeleine swings her legs. "We're making caramel apples today. I've never had one."

"Bring the fork to your mouth, dear, not the mouth to the fork. Pedro is still missing. The last time, Frank down the street called to say he was

30

eating from the trash. Stop swinging your legs. Why would he eat scraps when he has every kind of food he could want here?"

Madeleine stills her legs and brings the fork to her mouth. She cuts her pancakes into equal-sized pieces. In the corner of the shop, a briefer stack of pancakes sits in a bowl marked *Pedro*.

"He'll have to stay in the house when he gets back. This will give him anxiety attacks, but it's for his own good." Mrs. Santiago slides a sausage link into a pan of quivering grease. "Maybe it's time he started eating canine food."

"What about a leash?"

Mrs. Santiago snorts and gives the pan a shake. "He'd die on a leash." She brightens with a new thought. "Madeleine, it is almost your birthday. Who should we invite to your birthday dinner?"

Madeleine pretends the article she is reading is the most important article in the world. "No, thank you."

"You can't 'no, thank you' your birthday."

"You 'no, thank you'ed your last birthday."

"That's different." Mrs. Santiago wags a tube of sausage at her. "I'm old and allowed to ignore whatever I want, like time. How about Sandra?"

Sandra is Mrs. Santiago's sister, a retired reading specialist and paraplegic who tests Madeleine's aptitude by having her read Harlequin romances aloud.

Madeleine doesn't answer.

"What about Jill from school?"

"I hate Jill from school."

Mrs. Santiago makes the tsking sound that means she's offended and only half-listening. "Where did this hate come from? Your mother loved everything."

"Like what?" Madeleine says. This is her second favorite game.

"Flamingoes, your father, when people slipped. Not when they would fall outright and get hurt. When they would lose their footing for a second. She'd laugh so hard she'd turn purple."

Madeleine frowns. "I already know those."

"You ask every day, dear," Mrs. Santiago says.

It has been a year and a half since Madeleine lost her mother, and she has been living, more or less, alone. Her father owned several businesses in the city, among them a celebrated cheese store in the Ninth Street Market, but hasn't so much as sniffed a wheel of Roquefort since his wife's death. He stays in his room, listening to her favorite records. Not even the sound of his daughter calling his name can rouse him as each day passes seasonlessly by.

Madeleine knows she will only be getting a Christmas/birthday present from Mrs. Santiago and it will likely be a knit vest with a Pedro on it, while Pedro will receive a knit vest with a Madeleine on it. "I don't want a party," she says. "And that is that."

"I promised your mother. And that is that." Mrs. Santiago shrugs.

Madcleine shrugs.

Mrs. Santiago looks outside and gives a sudden wave. "The McCormicks are here. Get your things."

Madeleine stacks her plates in the silver sink. She presses her chin into Mrs. Santiago's elbow as the woman slices the browned sausage into medallions. Then she re-layers coat-scarf-hat by the door.

Outside, she exchanges vague *heys* with Jill McCormick and her two older brothers. Together, the children boot past the carousel horse (good-bye, horse), back down the alley, through the back doors of the bread store (cloths, earth smells), the fish shop (boxes on boxes stacked on boxes), the cooking store (a worker sitting on a crate peels a potato, cigarette balanced on his lip) and through another alley until they arrive at the immortal realization of Saint Anthony's.

Saint Anthony of the Immaculate Heart's schoolyard, the size of a football field, is shaped like an hourglass. On the top half (what time you have left), grades K to 4 double-Dutch and hop-scotch; on the bottom (what time you have lost) grades 5 to 8 hang in slack-jawed clots digging fingernails into their pimples. The middle belt section acts as repose for teachers who hand off whistles, balls, warnings, and gossip before diving back in.

Row homes, each bearing five families, border the field. Every morning out of these crowded brick houses emerge the sorriest kids in the world, yawning into maroon V-necks, sneering at each other to get off, stop it, find the cat, stop doing that to the cat, shut up, leave it, give it back! The proposition of the yard is conducted on an upward slant, so that children going to school can climb from their cruddy homes with plenty of time to appreciate the magnitude of the church and school. *Check me out,* the building says, *this is what happens for those who pray.* At the end of each learning day, the school dispenses the children back to their cruddy homes, quick as gravity.

Here is Madeleine, on the day of the caramel apples, blending in with these kids as they trudge to the schoolyard to engage in a perfunctory morning recess. Madeleine prefers to spend this and every recess alone, singing scales under her breath, walking laps up and down the parking lot. Madeleine has no friends: Not because she contains a tender grace that fifth graders detect and loathe. Not because she has a natural ability that points her starward, though she does. Madeleine has no friends because she is a jerk.

"Look alive, bubble butt," she said to Marty Welsh, who was dawdling at the pencil sharpener. That his parents had divorced the week before did not matter to Madeleine. An absent father doesn't give you the right to sharpen your pencil for, like, half an hour.

This is what Madeleine said to Jill McCormick (darting between her brothers, who swat at her) on the occasion of Jill's umpteenth attempt to befriend her: "Your clinginess is embarrassing."

Madeleine had one friend: Emily, a broad-shouldered ice skater who wound up at Saint Anthony's as the result of a clerical mistake. Once, Madeleine watched her make a series of circles on an ice rink. On solid ground, Emily still walked as if negotiating with a sliver of blade. Her parents moved to Canada so she could live closer to ice. Not before she taught Madeleine every curse word she knew, in the girls' bathroom on her last day, with reverence: *shit, cunt, piss, bitch*. Madeleine uses these words when one of her classmates tries to hang around, as in: *Get your piss cunt out of my creamy fucking way.*

There was a reprieve in her isolation in the weeks following her mother's death when Madeleine, polite with tragedy, allowed Jill to pal around. It wasn't long before she regained her wits and shooed her away.

Even jerks have mothers who die.

Into the thoughts of every playing child careens the clanging of an oversized bell, rung with gusto by Principal Randles. The children line up according to grade and height. Some of the older ones take their time. Principal Randles eyes these delinquents and rings harder. She will ring and ring until she achieves order. Until the kids standing closest to her clamp their hands over their ears. Madeleine is corralled into line by her homeroom teacher, Miss Greene. Finally, the ringing ends. A chrism of sweat shines on the principal's neck.

Miss Greene kneels next to Madeleine. On the stage of Madeleine's school-to-home world, Miss Greene is a main player. Madeleine has memorized every intonation of her teacher's voice, every possible way she wears her blunt, nut-colored hair, every time she has varied from her black sweater on black skirt wardrobe—twice. Miss Greene always smells like a tangerine and Madeleine likes that she never wears holiday-themed apparel like the other homeroom teacher, who today wears a holly-leaf tracksuit.

Miss Greene keeps her voice low. "Clare Kelly has been involved in an accident and won't be in today."

"What kind of accident?" Madeleine says.

"A serious one."

"Is she dead?"

"She's not dead." Miss Greene makes the expression that means: *That is a disrespectful question.* "I'd like you to sing 'Here I am, Lord' at this morning's mass."

"Has this been approved?" Madeleine doesn't clarify because she is daft or aggravating. She clarifies because she is a girl who has had things taken away. Even before her mother died, she was not a girl who assumed her train would come. Last year, for example, she delivered a perfect rendition of "On Eagle's Wings," and because of the shit show that happened afterward she had to sit in detention for a week.

Miss Greene's smile falters. "Approved."

Madeleine is overcome by the desire to cartwheel, which she overcomes. She wants to sing in church more than she wants a caramel apple. In the shadow of the building, they pray: a shower before entering the house after the beach. Amened, every other grade goes to their class-rooms. The fifth grade follows Principal Randles through the corridors to church. Two girls in, behind Maisie's confused spine, Madeleine tries to control her flopping, lurching heart.

Here I am, Lord. The lyrics batter Madeleine's brain. All holiness and thank you, Saint Karma, for injuring that plaited kiss-ass Clare Kelly. *I will hold your people in my heart.* Hit "I." Hit "people." Hold "heart," vibrato, done. Madeleine's big chance. Time to knock it out of the park, toots. Here I am, Lord. Check this fucking business out.

9:00 A.M.

*J*ack Francis Lorca, owner of The Cat's Pajamas and what are considered two of the finest ears in jazz, sits hunched on the side of a cot, staring into the uncurious dark. So dark he cannot tell if his eyes are open.

Someone is knocking on the front door, or it is a residual dream sound. Or a stray stone shaken loose from the rock of tinnitus. If it wants to be answered, Lorca thinks, it will have to come again.

In the club's heyday this room had been a kitchen, but now it is his office and makeshift sleeping quarters for his house musicians. Max Cubanista, bandleader, and Gray Gus Stein, drummer, slumber on the floor by his feet. Sonny Vega, rhythm guitarist and know-it-all, mumbles on his cot in the walk-in freezer. "Christian Street. Faster." Even in dreams, correcting someone's route across town.

Lorca has been sleeping here, nubby peacoat rolled for a pillow, because his apartment without Louisa seems dead. He does not remember particulars but is certain the constellation of shot glasses arranged around the bodies of his friends played a role in the headache blooming at the base of his skull. He is a man of average height. Not an attractive man but striking. The three names tattooed on his right arm are Francis, Alexander, and Louisa. The guitar tattooed on his left arm is a D'Angelico Snakehead, the same one that hangs over the bar like a prized swordfish. Lorca wears the same clothes from the previous day: black jeans and T-shirt, a narrow belt of fatigued leather. He bats at the wall for the switch that controls the overhead lamp and braces against the light.

The nucleus of the room is a round, battered table. Lorca's father, Francis, the bar's original owner, had bought it, still new, for what he called "family dinners," and around it many jazz greats had eaten, played cards, out-fish-taled each other. Now the table is covered with parts from the model plane Gray Gus has been negotiating with for weeks, its inner workings propped on empty spools to dry.

The oven is stuffed with old set lists. A glass vase filled with picks. Working and nonworking amps. A trash bag, marked, threateningly: *Christmas.* A woman's pearl-colored coat hangs over the back of a chair, too nice for the room.

It is almost a home.

The knocking on the front door returns, insists.

Lorca trudges shoeless through the darkened club. The rapping becomes more insistent. *I hear you,* he tells it. He hopes it is his son, Alex, who left without saying good-bye the night before. But instead a man in an unfortunate suit holds out a badge like an apology toward the peephole. His voice is close shaven. "Mr. Lorca?"

"We don't serve until noon," Lorca says.

The man shifts from foot to foot. "Hello?"

Lorca releases the chain and jolts the door open, revealing the cop and a scene of flurries.

"Is it snowing?" Lorca says to no one.

The cop consults the sky. "Since dawn."

Lorca pulls a pack of cigarettes from his back pocket and shakes one out. "In here it's always midnight. I guess you want to come in." He motions for the man to pass him, then follows him into the club.

The club has a carved-out quality like the caboose of a train. A knee-high step separates the room from the stage, where, amid an argument of cables, Gray Gus's drum set sits, charred. The stools lining the long oak bar are draped in unlit twinkle lights. Lorca recalls a boozy, predawn idea of hanging them. He had overturned chairs on only half of the tables before quitting, he recalls, to get sick in the men's bathroom. The Snakehead, a 1932 archtop with Waverly individual tuners, is the club's beating heart. Lorca's father said he won it in an arm-wrestling match but this was one of his fish tales. He had saved for years to buy it. Next to his picture a sign reads: *All musicians are liars except you and me and I'm not so sure about you.*

The back of the cop's collar is not fully folded

over his tie. "I don't want to take up much of your time," he says.

"Then don't." Lorca plugs the lights in. "Ta-da." They go green then red then blue. "When's the last time we had a white Christmas?"

"It's not likely to last." The cop extends his hand and they shake. "Len Thomas." He shows his badge again.

Lorca nods toward it. "Jack Francis Lorca."

The cop pulls a notebook from his blazer pocket. "I'm afraid we've gotten several calls about your club. Over capacity, use of pyrotechnics, excessive smoke . . ."

"Where's Renaldo? Normally they send him."

Len scribbles into his notebook. "Renaldo got promoted."

"Good for him. Deserves it. Excessive smoke?" Lorca says. "The crème brûlée torch?"

The cop points to Gus's drums. The warped cymbals hang on blackened stands. A singed, licorice smell emanates from them.

"He wanted to see if every time he hit the cymbals, flames would explode," Lorca says.

"Did it work?"

"Not like we thought it would," Lorca admits.

The cop reads from his notebook. ". . . Consistent refusal to abide by the city's law of no smoking inside the premises."

Lorca stubs out his cigarette in one of the bar's ashtrays. "I can't get used to that law."

41

"It was passed in 2007."

"Has it been that long? We're all getting so old."

". . . Consistent refusal to stop serving alcohol at two A.M. I stopped in last night around three and saw fifty or so people cheering on a drummer dousing his drum set in lighter fluid."

"If you think about it," Lorca says, "it's funny." The cop's expression doesn't budge. "I'll tell Gus no more fires."

"That's not all, Mr. Lorca. This property"—he points to the garbage bags, the stage—"is licensed as a bar, and a bar only. No one is legally allowed to use this property as a residence. How many people stay here every night, Mr. Lorca?"

The shape of the cop's visit and the potential price tag form in Lorca's mind. For years Renaldo let them go on all of it. Being exposed as a residence would be thousands of dollars. As long as the boys stay sleeping in the back, he can bargain this cop down. He raises his hands as if guilty. "I've been crashing here," he says. "My girlfriend and I have hit upon hard times."

The cop raises one eyebrow. "No one else?"

Sonny emerges from the back room. His hastily tied robe reveals his pale, hairless chest. A lit cigarette hangs from his lips. His slippers make hard scuffling sounds. He mutely acknowledges Len as he passes. "We got any eggs? We're out in the back." He checks the bar's fridge and straightens up, holding a carton of orange juice.

Lorca says, "This is Len Thomas. He's here because he's gotten several calls about our club." He turns to the cop. "This is Sonny Vega; he's here because he has nowhere else to go."

"You look familiar," Sonny says. "Who do we know?"

"I doubt we have mutual friends." The cop affects a cool lean but misses the bar with his elbow. He tries again while Sonny smokes and watches.

"There're only two kinds of people in this city," Sonny says. "Those who know each other and those who haven't figured out yet how they know each other."

"I'm from Boston," the cop says.

"Well, hell." Sonny gives a look to Lorca: *I tried.*

"Let's talk this out," Lorca says. "I'll make eggs."

"Mr. Lorca, you've received seven visits from Officer Renaldo. The time for talking is over." The cop flips the notebook shut and hands Lorca a citation the color of emergency cones. Lorca scans it to locate the total. "You're kidding."

Sonny reads over his shoulder. "Holy shit."

"You have thirty days to pay," the cop says, looking satisfied. "I'll be coming every night to check that the city's ordinances are being respected. Another infraction and it's your bar."

Lorca follows as the cop strides through the

43

vestibule, jolts open the front door, and turns. The flurries have lost their ambition, but the visit seems to have emboldened him. "Play by the rules, Mr. Lorca, or it's your bar."

Something about this man's plumped-up face, the thought of pulling another T-shirt out of his duffel bag, the impending holiday, calcifies in Lorca. "Do you think this is fair?" he says. "Coming into a club with a list of infractions and a fee that, let's be honest, there is very little chance I can come up with."

"It's not my choice," Len says.

"It's not your choice."

"Well, it's not."

"I'm not asking that. I'm asking if you think it's fair."

A truck karangs by. The cop waits for it to pass. "Mr. Lorca," he stammers.

"Call me Jack," Lorca says. "Only my friends call me Lorca."

Len Thomas opens his mouth to speak, but Lorca shuts the door. Pain pauses him in the vestibule by the stack of phone books. Though he is only forty, some unkind rod is normally clanging against his wrists and knees. A woman in his inner ear canal holds a relentless, intimate C and he is always shaking his head to clear her.

Lorca has never been a player but can tell even in recordings whether a guitarist is well rested or angry, where the piano is located in the studio.

44

When he was a little boy, his father would choose a piano key at random, and Lorca would call out the note; correctly, every time. Charged by this special rite, his ears are virtuoso in shape. Well-formed lobes make lowercase *j*'s against his sideburns. Pert, stubborn tragus. When Lorca is engaged in listening, and he is always listening, his eyes and mouth harden and conspire toward his sharp nose, making him appear cruel.

Sonny sits at the bar, staring at the citation. "Are we screwed?"

Lorca's hand fumbles on a lighter. It takes him three tries to get his cigarette lit. "I'll call Uncle Ray for the money."

"You realize that's illegal," Sonny says, about the cigarette.

"Everything is illegal."

"Where's Renaldo when you need him?"

Lorca holds the citation up to the light, as if it might be counterfeit. The impossible total. "Renaldo got promoted," he says.

"Good for him," Sonny says. "Deserves it."

Lorca shakes his head. "Len Thomas from Boston."

"You know what they say." Sonny pulls mournfully from the carton of orange juice. "Never trust a man with two first names."

10:00 A.M.

*P*rincipal Randles halts, startling the height-ordered line that follows her.

"Children," she says. "You should want to do right by the Lord. When you pray you should feel overcome by a sense of purity and rightness. The equivalent of lighting a white candle in a white room." She lights an invisible candle with an invisible match. "Except . . ." She blows out the invisible match. "You are the white room and what's inside you is the white candle."

It is the same speech she made before Madeleine's class received the sacrament of Reconciliation, unburdening themselves of every *goddamn,* and Confirmation, when the Holy Spirit said, *Oh there you are, I see you*. Madeleine did not feel like a white room during either of those sacraments but assumes she will when it's time for the next one, Matrimony. Madeleine is double-bolt positive that every married couple is happy.

Principal Randles throws open the door to the church and ushers the children into pews to practice being white rooms. Madeleine flattens her back against the hard wood and waits to be overcome by light. Here it comes, she thinks. But it is a yawn. She smells the pine scent of mahogany cleaner. Her thoughts return to singing. Hit, hold, vibrato. She forgets to want to be a white room.

Sunshine swells into the church. How the stained-glass windows screw with it, cutting the light into shapes and hurling them around! An orange triangle on the donations box. Lavender octagons on an altar boy's vestments. Madeleine doesn't understand decimals but she knows red, orange, yellow, green, blue, purple make a rainbow.

Around her, a group *Amen*. She has missed a prayer. Everyone crosses themselves. Everyone glances around for what now. "And now," Father Gary announces, "Clare Kelly will lead us in the responsorial song."

Miss Greene pads onto the altar's carpet and whispers into Father Gary's ear. He forgets the microphone. "Is she dead?" Frantic explaining. "Madeleine Altimari?" He pronounces her last name as if somewhere there is another, more innocuous Madeleine.

The fifth grade's morning mass daze is punctured by this development. They turn shocked faces to Madeleine, who unceremoniously climbs over them to reach the aisle.

Principal Randles goose-steps onto the altar. She and Miss Greene hold a muted, brief debate. Madeleine freezes in the aisle. The children squirm in their pews. The microphone catches a few words. "Assembly . . . unpleasant."

The knot of teacher/principal/priest untangles,

leaving Father Gary to announce the call into the microphone: Madeleine Altimari.

In her relief, Madeleine forgets to go slow, kneel, genuflect, bow at the cross, or acknowledge the priest. She races to the microphone, narrowly avoiding Miss Greene, who attempts to give her a good-luck pat. The organist plays a plucky intro. Madeleine makes it to the podium. *Here I go, Mama.* She plants her child size twelves into the altar's plush. Every child in every pew leans forward. The organist winds down the intro. Madeline opens her mouth to sing.

"Here I am!" Clare Kelly step-crutches up the aisle, her arm tucked into a sling and her parents trailing. "I can sing!" she says, reaching the front. The organist stops playing. Madeleine's mouth, poised in an angelic O, shuts.

"A miracle!" Principal Randles jumps from her seat, applauding. Sarina protests. The principal asks, will Miss Greene join her in the back hall near the statue and the vigil candles? There she explains that while it was remarkable, exemplary even, worthy of Student of the Week if that ribbon hadn't already been written out to Clare, that Madeleine was willing to step in at the last minute, when they thought Clare would be an unintelligible mess for days, but Clare is here, telligible, with her parents, the same parents who last year financed the building of this back hall, that statue, and these vigil candles. "It's the daughter of all this." She gestures around the hall. "Versus the daughter of a prostitute."

Sarina removes her glasses. Two red stars appear on her cheeks. "Madeleine's mother was not a prostitute."

"Dancer," Principal Randles says.

"Not the same," Sarina says.

"It's settled!" Principal Randles throws up her hands and returns to the Kellys with bright eyes.

Sarina scans the aisle for Madeleine, but the girl has already returned to her pew and is watching Clare step-crutch onto the altar toward the microphone.

Sarina takes her place next to her grade partner. "Isn't she an angel?" the woman says, meaning Clare.

The organist restarts the intro. Clare opens her mouth to sing.

10:30 A.M.

*T*he first thing Ray asks when he answers the phone is whether the roof he installed in 1985 is intact. When Lorca assures him it is, Ray delivers a sermon on The Importance of a Sturdy Roof. ". . . The plumbing will rot, the floors will join them, but I used the best materials money could buy on that roof." Lorca listens, sitting amid the wreckage of Gus's model plane. Flaps, wheels, the fuselage, emergency doors. Ray runs a construction company in Reading that employs wanderers and harmless crooks. "I loved your father a lot. Jackie?" Ray interrupts himself. "How much trouble are you in?"

"Am I that obvious?" Lorca says.

Lorca hears laughing, then the unmistakable sound of nose spray. "Only one reason to call Reading."

Lorca tells him about the citation and asks for the money.

"Can't do it, buddy," Ray says. "They slaughtered me."

Blood evacuates Lorca's ears and cheeks. He doesn't know who "they" are. They could be the government, the union, the clattering aunts on Ray's wife's side who take dazed, hospitalizing falls twice a year.

"I always thought it'd be Max who'd run the club into the ground," Ray says. "Always disappearing. Showing up with this girl or that."

"That would have been what they call a safe bet," Lorca says.

"At least you don't have to spray a boatload of chemicals up your nose every second," Ray says. "Be thankful for your health. And Alex and Louisa. You still smoking?"

Lorca says he is.

"Maybe quit. Do you pray?"

"I don't," Lorca says.

"Maybe start." More coughing. This time Ray is laughing. "Why did the cop come today?" he says. "As opposed to last week, or never?"

Lorca rolls a plane wheel over the table. "Last night," he says. "We set fire to Gus's drum set and someone called the cops."

The purgatory of his uncle's silence follows. "Why would you do something like set fire to a drum set?"

Lorca wants to bring his fist down in the middle of the table and send the plane's pieces hurtling into the dirty walls. The tail is separate from the body. The cockpit arranged at an awkward angle to dry. Lorca has asked Gus several times to get rid of the plane. He gets nervous around delicate things.

"Louisa left," Lorca says. "I wanted to see something"—he rests his forehead against the hard wood of the table—"bright."

51

11:10 A.M.

The twenty-four children of Miss Greene's art class wear twenty-four Santa hats and color twenty-four pictures of Santa. Each child's name is spelled in glitter on the cotton brim of his or her hat. The classroom smells like fish and damp lunches.

Because the seats are arranged by height order and because when it comes to height Madeleine is nothing special, she sits in the third row, first desk, coloring and giving herself pep talks. Her mother taught her not to dwell so Madeleine cheers herself by replaying the moment in the third chorus of "Here I am, Lord," when Clare squeaked on the word *I*.

Clare colors her Santa methodically, using classic hues: scarlet for the coat, white for the trim, forest green for the holly leaf that hangs above his head. When she needs red for Santa's cheeks, she muscles the crayon from diabetic Duke's hand.

In the space next to Santa's outline, Madeleine lists songs she will practice later. "Take the A Train," "Hey There." At least there will be caramel apples. Madeleine spies them on the craft table, covered by a festive sheet.

Each child has been guaranteed one apple to

cajole and twist through a pot of caramel. Madeleine will suffer through the hundreds of questions her classmates will ask about each step. She will lay her coated apple with the care of a surgeon on a sheet of wax paper to dry. She will not sprinkle it with peanut butter chips or walnuts or rainbow sprinkles. She has never had a caramel apple and wants a pure experience.

At the front of the room, Miss Greene clears her throat for their attention.

"It is eleven eleven," she informs them. "Make a wish."

The children of Homeroom 5A bow their heads and wish. Madeleine discards hers—*May Clare Kelly get laryngitis*—so she can watch Miss Greene. When her head is bowed her soft hair reaches her collarbone. What do fifth-grade teachers wish for?

Miss Greene claps to signal the end of wishing. The school nurse has appeared and wants everyone to listen to her. Madeleine assumes she is there to administer the apples.

"Lice," she declares, "are bugs that live in your hair."

Several of the girls give their pony- and pigtails vague tugs. The nurse snaps gloves on and asks them to line up. "We'll go one by one."

The first to go is Denny Pennypack, who with his brothers and sisters maintains a multigrade bullying contingent. The Pennypacks keep at least five smaller children in tow at any given recess. The purpose of these children seems to be to congratulate the Pennypacks and to offer them a stray glove or scarf if one of the Pennypacks forgets theirs. These children are for parts. If she were interested in minions Madeleine would be a bully, but she doesn't like weak people hanging around.

Every Sunday in Saint Anthony's Church, Mr. and Mrs. Pennypack hand over their contribution in a bright pink envelope. The Pennypack mansion takes up a city block and is visible from the back windows of Saint Anthony's. Around it, miles of row homes like soiled clouds.

The nurse digs around in Denny's hair until she is satisfied. Then Jill goes. Madeleine feels bad for Jill, whose two older brothers keep her in a constant state of fear. Then the Anderson twin. Yawn. Then the other Anderson twin. Double yawn. Then the girl Madeleine always wants to call Lynn who is actually Leigh. Then Brie whose real name is Brianna, but they already had a Brianna. One by one, each kid puts their head under the searching fingers of the nurse then goes back to their drawing.

It is Madeleine's turn. The nurse sifts and stops. "This one." She takes hold of Madeleine's elbow and steers her toward the hallway. "Please go see Principal Randles."

"Can I get my list?" Madeleine says.

"Your what?"

"Nose has bugs in her hair!" Denny clutches his stomach with glee.

Miss Greene tells Denny to stop laughing, but he is addicted to his classmates' scared tittering. He fakes falling out of his chair with delight. More fearful tittering. More play-acting.

Miss Greene walks Madeleine to Principal Randles's office and instructs her to sit on the pew outside. She whispers a few words to the secretary, then kneels so she is the same height as Madeleine.

"Don't listen to that jackass Denny Pennypack," she says.

Madeleine has never heard a teacher curse before. Miss Greene high-heels back to class and Madeleine waits on the hard bench.

After what feels like an hour, the secretary tells her that no one is answering the phone at her house. "Where is your father?"

Madeleine thinks of the phone chiming from the kitchen into her father's bedroom, where he no doubt dozes to an old record. At one time, he was the most respected vendor on Ninth Street. Now, the sound of the oven door scares him.

"How should I know?" Madeleine can feel the bugs sliding down strands of her hair. She can feel them in her ears, setting up permanent housing. She can feel them burrowing deeper, possibly into her brain. Laughter jangles down the hall from her classroom. She cranes her neck to see inside. Will they save an apple for her? They seem to be cleaning up.

"Am I getting a caramel apple or what?"

The sound of her voice jolts the secretary out of her paperwork. "You'll have to ask the principal, Madeleine."

"I've been waiting forever. Where is she?"

"Here I am, Madeleine." Principal Randles appears in the doorway. She squats so she is the same height as Madeleine. Most adults do this so they don't appear menacing. "When everyone else goes home for lunch, you will go home and stay home," she says. "Show this to your father." She thrusts a comb and a piece of paper into Madeleine's hands and seems to think this is all the information the girl needs.

"Do I get an apple?" Madeleine says.

"Maybe Santa will bring you a caramel apple."

"Santa doesn't exist." Madeleine dismisses this idea with a wave of her hand. "I feel I should be allowed to get my drawing."

"I feel I should win a million dollars," Principal Randles says.

"I don't know how that applies to me," Madeleine says. "Did someone eat my apple?"

"You shouldn't be thinking about apples. You should be thinking about getting the bugs out of your hair."

"I made one for her." Miss Greene stands in the

56

doorway holding Madeleine's schoolbag in one hand and in the other, an apple covered in dried caramel. Miss Greene can draw the best giraffes. An apple made by Miss Greene is a perfect apple. Behind her, Denny Pennypack smirks. One of the many baffling situations at Saint Anthony's is his position as hall monitor, enabling him to be anywhere at any time.

Madeleine takes the apple from Miss Greene. She can see no flaw or seam in its caramel coat.

"You have your apple. Go before your sass gets you in trouble and tell your father to buy that shampoo," Principal Randles says. She and Miss Greene turn away.

With a juvenile delinquent's knack for timing, Denny karate-chops Madeleine's apple off the stick, sending it hurtling across the hall where it collides against a display of student papers answering the question: *Could World War II have been prevented?* Principal Randles and Miss Greene wheel around. The apple sits in a pile of pencil dust and hall dirt. Madeleine can see where the wall forced a mottled wound on its otherwise perfect surface.

"She threw her apple against the wall!" Denny exclaims. "The lice must be making her crazy!"

Madeleine balls up her fists. "This is fucking bullshit!" She glares at Principal Randles. "This turd did that on purpose, are you blind?"

The principal's mouth falls open. Madeleine is

still going. Bitch rag, she tells her. Colossal prick munch.

"Expelled," Principal Randles chokes.

Denny snorts with pleasure. Madeleine bridges the distance between them in two steps. She remembers to bring her arm back like a slingshot and to keep her thumb out of the fist she plants on Denny's mug. Denny's nose explodes and releases admirable waves of blood. It can't get enough of releasing itself, it's wild over it. Madeleine marvels at how much blood he is able to produce. By the end of the commotion, his nose is wrapped in bandages and Miss Greene is escorting Madeleine speedily down the yellow hallway. Each grade's efforts at Christmas cheer take up the walls. The third grade's assignment seemed to be: Do as much damage as you can with green crayons. Madeleine exits the school amid these violent displays.

The other students file out of their classrooms. They will go to their homes for lunch and are expected to be back within one hour. Those whose parents aren't home during the day have made arrangements with other families. Those with no arrangements sit in the cafeteria and eat dry sandwiches under the semiwatchful eye of a teacher who drew the shortest straw.

"I wish you hadn't done that," Miss Greene says.

"I wanted to sing." Madeleine shifts underneath

the weight of her backpack, then walks away. She can tell Miss Greene is watching her because she hasn't heard her teacher's high heels signal an exit. It occurs to Madeleine that she could cry, but she sings instead.

You must take the A train
to go to Sugar Hill, way up in Harlem

Harlem is the crown on top of Manhattan, New York City. Billie Holiday was a singer who squandered her gift on drugs. Madeleine knows this the same way she knows keeping your thumb inside your fist when you punch someone is a good way to break your thumb. Because her mother taught her.

Sarina watches Madeleine walk away, her flamingo backpack slouched over her shoulder. For a moment, she had been able to see past the girl's rough exterior to something squirming and hurt. Sarina is a nonpracticing everything, so Christmas is no more than a day off with Chinese food, or a drive to visit her sister and her bleached-looking family. But it is Madeleine's holiday. Tears push into her eyes. A measly apple.

Sarina returns to her classroom and listens to the message from her ex, Marcos. He will be in the city tonight, does she want to meet?

Through the window she can see Principal Randles standing amid the tributaries of retreating students, correcting attitude and posture as they stream by. Her hawkish nose, the surprisingly dainty waist. Always some oozing sandwich for lunch: egg, crab, or tuna salad. Sarina makes the mistake of assuming every principal is good, every teacher selfless, but what kind of principal expels a little girl the year her mother died?

Sarina deletes the message, thinking of key lime pie.

11:30 A.M.

Alex Lorca enters the club: hollering, clapping, popping his knuckles, kissing Sonny on the cheek, kissing his father on the cheek. Always with Alex these days is the girlfriend, dress half off, lips pouting around a Parliament. Alex sings. Tonight! Most holy, sacred night! Alex pretends to play a drum set that explodes, he pretends he is exploding too, grabs onto his girl who shrieks at him to get off. She has a name like Aruna Sha. Her name is Aruna Sha. They are sixteen and skinny. Their collarbones vault in upsetting directions.

Alex gives the Snakehead a reverent tap. He insists on being treated like a man yet maintains a boy's tendency to test the height of every hanging thing. He pummels Lorca with fake punches. "It snowed, Pops," he says.

"It's done, though," Aruna says.

"Aruna left her coat here last night."

"It's silk," she says.

"Ooh la la," says Sonny.

Alex's cheeks are flushed the same color as the scarf he wears winter or summer. The same shade as Aruna's lipstick: fire hydrant red. These kids are the only colors in the bar. "Tonight's the night."

"I give up," Lorca says. "Why is tonight the night?"

"I'm playing with the Cubanistas. You said." More punches, more snapping. Sonny and Lorca exchange a glance. Alex goes to the back to retrieve the coat. They hear him in the hall, yes-yesing and slapping his thighs.

Aruna scrutinizes her nails. "Is there a salon around here? Is there anything around here besides warehouses?" She pulls a cigarette from a purse tucked under her armpit and lights it.

Sonny says, "There's no smoking in here, honey."

Her gaze slides from the ashtrays to the floor, where last night's cigarettes are murdered. "We were smoking last night."

"It's a new day, I guess," Sonny says.

She drops it, kills it. Alex returns with the coat and places it over her shoulders with a delicacy that surprises Lorca. Alex lives in the suburbs with his mother but is forever escaping to the city, begging to stay with his father, begging to play at the club. "You think Max will let me solo or will I just be backing tonight? He'll let me solo once, maybe?"

Sonny sighs. Alex reads his face and turns to his father. "What'd I miss?"

"You're underage," Lorca says.

Alex laughs. "I was underage last night too, when you promised."

"A cop came by this morning—" Sonny begins, but Lorca interrupts him. "Things have changed,"

62

he says. "Last night I said you could play. Now you can't. I said I was *sorry*."

The mirth in Alex's face vanishes and a murkier expression replaces it—the one Lorca is more accustomed to evoking in his son. "You didn't say you were *sorry*."

"Of course I'm sorry!" Lorca's tone is rougher than he wants. He tries to think of something softer to say. Alex lifts Sonny's guitar from the table and takes a seat, his back toward the men. Aruna sits in the chair next to him. She thrusts a lip toward a compact and reglosses it while he noodles around a melody.

Francis taught Alex how to hold his guitar the way Django Reinhardt did, like the guys in Italy and Spain do, forward on his knee like he was playing to it. It reminds Lorca of Babe Ruth, pointing his bat to left field. Lorca watches him pin chords to the neck. Django was his Spider-Man. When he was nine Alex read that Django played every gig wearing a scarf, and he had worn one ever since. He slept clutching his guitar like a teddy bear. Lorca misses his father so acutely that for a moment he is unable to gather breath.

Alex settles on a melody.

"Is that 'Troublant Bolero'?" Lorca says. "When did you learn that?"

Alex ignores him. Expressionless, he picks through the hardest progression, staring at the wall. Suddenly disgusted, he returns the guitar to its case. This jag will go on for a day. Lorca innately knows his son's moods and tendencies the way you know on a flight, even with your eyes closed, that a plane is banking.

Aruna shuts her compact and replaces the cap to her lipstick. She is a little girl with a lot of eyeliner, Lorca thinks. He tugs a twenty from his pocket and thrusts it toward his son. Alex pushes past him into the vestibule. "Let's go," he says to Aruna.

Lorca hands the money to her. "Get dinner tonight. You both look like skeletons."

"I will." She folds the bill into her bag and touches the snarled twinkle lights. "Are you going to hang these up today?"

Lorca nods. "That's the plan."

She looks up to the tin ceiling, the eaves, the walls. "It'll be awful pretty when you do." It startles Lorca how different she looks when she smiles. It seems to hit Sonny too. The men straighten up.

"Merry Christmas," she says.

"Merry Christmas," they say. Then, in the direction of the front door, Lorca calls: "Merry Christmas, son."

Alex's voice sulks in from the vestibule. "It's not Christmas yet."

"He told all our friends," Aruna says, ". . . is the thing."

They leave. Lorca and Sonny watch them walk away through the window. Jeans and sneakers. Aruna's floral dress with winter boots. Then the window returns to the gray static of the street. A stray flurry.

Alex's mother had been a casual girlfriend of Lorca's. When she found out she was pregnant, he vowed to pay half of everything. When he couldn't, his father made up the difference. Or, Sonny did. Or, after they started dating, Louisa. Alexander was the strongest name Lorca could think of and Alex grew up strong, even if he was a little bratty, a little hurt.

"Why didn't you tell him?" Sonny says.

"I don't want him to worry."

"That worked well, then."

"We tell no one," Lorca says. "Not Alex or Gus or Max. Not Valentine." He knows keeping it quiet will be as hard as getting the money. Gab is what Sonny likes to do most besides play.

"Nail place!" Sonny slaps the inside of his wrist. "Girard and Susquehanna!" He clamors to catch them. The heavy click of the door.

Lorca pulls himself a pint. He fishes out the last egg from the fridge and cracks it into the beer. The citation shines on his desk in the back. He uses it as a coaster. A watery ring grows and dilutes the cop's signature.

He picks up the phone by his elbow and dials. After a few rings her machine clicks on. Even her recorded voice unmoors him. He coughs for the first few minutes of his message. He says, "A Good Morning is what you used to call an egg cracked into a beer, right?" Drinking at barely noon will not refute her claim that he spends too much time at the club. "It's almost Christmas," he tries. His voice is not the one he wants. He shores it up before he speaks again, searching the room for anything helpful: the citation, Gus's unfinished plane, Sonny's crisp, folded bedsheets. There was a joke years ago that had her howling, but he can only remember the punch line.

He says, "You know damn well I can't read."

12:30 P.M.

Would it be okay for Sarina to come to the dinner they discussed that morning, over the pie, in the flurries, at the place?

Georgie says yes into the phone as if she has been waiting all morning for Sarina to call.

"What can I bring?" Sarina says. "You sure don't need pie."

"Yourself," she says. "Only yourself."

"Who will be there? How many people, I mean?" Sarina stutters. "So I know what to bring."

"Me, Bella, and her new girlfriend, Claudia. Pepper, get down! That's my cat. She jumped on the table. When I'm on the phone she thinks I'm talking to her."

"Bella and her girlfriend . . ." Sarina reminds her.

"She's like a furry human being. It's true what they say."

"It is," Sarina says.

"So true." Georgie sighs.

"Is that all then? Those are the only people coming?"

"Bella, Claudia, Ben and Annie of course, Michael. He just bought a ridiculous car."

Of course, Ben and Annie! Because married

people are always together! Sarina wants to retract her acceptance, the phone call, this day, like the cord to her vacuum that rewinds with a powerful *thwip!* How had she forgotten the pleasure of a carpet sucked clean? Vacuuming is how she'd prefer to spend the evening. Then a few hours at her easel. "So great," Sarina says, not specifying what would be great: a new car, seeing everyone, pie . . .

"Everyone will be thrilled to see you. What changed your mind?"

Everyone. Sarina hears the bell that signals the end of lunch. Through the window, she watches her students return dully to the yard. She injects her voice with an improbable amount of positivity. "I wanted to be in the company of adults."

"I'll help you find some." Georgie laughs, no doubt holding a fistful of roots, orbited by an adoring, whimsically colored cat. She is the kind of woman who is endlessly in from the garden where she has been cutting chives. "When was the last time we all saw each other? It's sad if you let yourself think about it."

"So sad," Sarina says.

"You will call if you are running late?"

"Of course!" She hangs up the phone.

In the yard children from several grades seem to be playing a game called Everyone Is Dying and There Is Chaos. One of them, an official-looking boy, barks orders, while someone else

68

yells "Mark" over and over. "I'm dead," a little girl says, before another voice corrects her: "You're not dead if you're talking." Through it all a kindergartener keeps up an impressive, enduring wail.

The game heightens as several kids scream contradictory directions. *Mark! Mark! Mark! Mark!*

Unless they really are dying, Sarina thinks, not rising from her desk.

1:00 P.M.

Madeleine sulks through the backyards of the row homes that border Saint Anthony's, past the market dotted with shoppers, to where Beauty Land sits, painted an unnatural pink, on a stretch of paved lot.

Darla Henshaw, junior hairdresser and default receptionist, is on the phone warning a client they can squeeze her in but the shampooers are already backed up. "Be ready to wait is what I'm telling you."

Madeleine hands Darla the piece of paper. Darla reads it as, in her ear, the client has her say. Darla says she gets it, it's hard all around, then hangs up. "Christ, Madeleine, lice?"

At the back of the salon, Vince Sherry, owner of Beauty Land, instructs his client to cover her eyes. He sprays her head in patient, liberal strokes. When the mist settles, he unwraps a stick of bubble gum and admires his work. "You're done, gorgeous. You look like three million dollars." Then he yells toward the front, "Who has lice?"

"I got expelled," Madeleine tells Darla.

"For having lice?" she says.

"For punching a boy."

"Madeleine punched a boy because she had lice!" Darla yells.

70

"The lice is unrelated," Madeleine says. "It's not my lucky day."

"No kidding." Vince appears at the desk. "You got lice and expelled. I wouldn't buy a lottery ticket."

Darla holds out a plastic bag. "Your scarf and hat. In here. We'll wash them."

Vince leads Madeleine to the bank of sinks and lifts her into the last chair. "Lice means you have good hair." He selects the particular shampoo from a top shelf and gestures to the older women who surround them; helmeted, curlered, flipping through brightly colored magazines. "These women would kill to have enough hair for lice."

When he is finished washing her hair, Vince escorts Madeleine to his station. He pumps the chair several times so she can see herself in the mirror. "We'll cut it, too," he says. "You're due."

Darla hovers nearby. "You'll never believe what they found in some reject's apartment in University City." The phone at the front desk rings. She leaves to answer it with an aggravated sigh.

Vince snips around Madeleine's ears. He was her mother's best friend and had promised to cut Madeleine's hair until she turned eighteen. Thin and mustached, he is the type to dart in place, several irons and dryers firing at once. Before the city's laws changed, he cut hair with a cigarette dangling from his mouth, cottony ash inches from Madeleine's cheek. Now, he chews gum while participating in an argument he's been having with Darla for as long as Madeleine can remember. The smell of him, conditioning crèmes and piney talc, has such a leveling effect on her that when she encounters these scents in other places she grows immediately calm.

Darla is back. She speaks so everyone in the salon can hear her. "A fucking alligator and a tiger."

"You didn't hear that," Vince says to Madeleine. Then, to Darla: "An alligator and a tiger what?" And Darla says, "Is what they found in this reject's apartment in University City."

The woman in the chair next to Madeleine flips a page in her magazine. "It's like the punch line to a joke," she says. "An alligator and a tiger."

"What kind of asshole," Darla asks, "keeps an alligator and a tiger in his apartment?" The ringing of the phone summons her to the front.

"You didn't hear that either." Vince clips and frowns. "What's up with the expulsion?"

"Denny Pennypack laughed at me and I punched him."

"You got expelled for that?" Vince peels another piece of gum from its pack. "Vicky Randles was so jealous of your mother she couldn't walk straight."

Madeleine never tires of this story. How Principal Randles and her mother went to school together. How everyone wanted to date her father. How her mother could dance better than all the neighborhood girls. How Vince and her father and mother built soapbox cars and raced them in Vet stadium's wide, flat parking lot. Before they were her father and mother. When they were just kids in snow hats.

"Mrs. Santiago stopped in to invite us to your birthday party," Vince says. "How old are you turning?"

"The God's honest truth is I would prefer not to be bothered. Mrs. Santiago is so overbearing."

Vince straightens up, suddenly livid. "Darla! Where are my tiny shears?"

"On your table, you drunk SOB! Try opening your eyes."

Vince digs through his drawers and Madeleine reads a magazine. On a beach on the other side of the world, people who are famous for who they are related to eat shellfish.

The woman in the chair next to her clucks her tongue. Her black hair is being highlighted the color of toast, the ends battened into squares of aluminum, making her look like a Martian. "You sound like an ungrateful little girl," she says. "Mrs. Santiago is a good woman."

Darla returns, plucks a pair of shears from Vince's tray, and holds them up. "What are these?"

"Those weren't there before!" Vince says.

"Your ass."

Vince resumes cutting Madeleine's hair and Madeleine tries not to stare at the woman whose insult has brought tears to her eyes.

"Don't mind Louisa," Vince says. "She's going through a transitional period. From bartender to question mark."

"Principal Randles said I was a problem child," Madeleine says.

"Just like your mom," he says. "Walk the line, girl. Or it's the strip club for you. And your mother would land right here"—Vince points to a tray of combs—"and beat the snot out of me."

"Fierce mother," the Martian says.

"My mother is dead," Madeleine says. This has the desired effect of changing the woman's smug expression to something resembling pity.

"She's Mark Altimari's kid," Vince says.

"Sugar," the woman says. "I'm sorry. I worked with your mother at The Courtland Avenue Club."

"Are you a snake lady?" Madeleine says.

"I was a snake lady. I work at The Cat's Pajamas now. Well, worked."

"What's The Cat's Pajamas?" Madeleine says.

"A jazz club."

"Jazz club?" Madeleine sits up abruptly, sending the magazine to the ground. "Where is it?"

"Jodi Columbo's here!" Darla yells from the front.

"I'm getting washed!" says Jodi. "Then I'm coming to see you, Vince."

"I wait with bated breath." Vince starts the hair dryer. Madeleine can't hear anything over its din. "Stop squirming or I'm going to burn your ears off." When her hair is dry he rotates the chair so she can see herself in the mirror. "Check out that pretty girl."

The ends of her hair brush her ears. The coarse bangs.

"Here's the deal." Vince hands her a paper bag. "Take this shampoo home and use it until it's gone. Every day. Don't throw it out before you use it all, and don't think you can skip it and trick me." He dusts stray hair from her neck as they walk to the front. When they reach the desk, Darla says, "The tiger ate the alligator, is how they found him."

Vince says, "The guy with the alligator?"

Darla swipes at her frosted bangs. "The asshole with the alligator. Only the tiger is still alive and the guy wants it back because he says the tiger and the alligator were his best friends."

"Takes all kinds," says Vince.

"I'll say," Darla says. Then, to Madeleine: "It's paid for. Get out of here."

Madeleine replaces her boots. Vince zips her coat. "Straight home," he says. "Don't punch any boys on the way." He grimaces toward the windows. "Is it getting dark already? It was light for like five minutes today."

Darla rolls her eyes. "Welcome to winter?"

Madeleine leaves. The door slams in bells. Outside on the cracked pavement her breath billows around her. Above her, the painted pink sign bleats against the sky: BEAUTY LAND. She pulls on her mittens and considers her next step.

In the endless array of mirrors, one thousand Darlas follow one thousand Vinces back to his station. She reads questions aloud from a magazine's holiday survey. Jodi is already sitting in Vince's chair, thin hair washed and held in a clip.

"What would you most like to find under the tree?" Darla reads.

"I'd like to find some goddamned time to think," Jodi says.

Vince says, "A TV that doesn't go out every time a plane flies by." He asks Louisa what she wants for Christmas. Louisa says, "I don't want anything, I'm fine."

"You have the disease my mother had," says Jodi. "Nice-itis."

"Is it contagious?" Vince says. "You should rub against Darla."

"You know what I want," Darla says. "You know what I really, really want?"

Vince says, "Tell us already."

Darla speaks with gravity. "I want to see Mark Recchi coming out to get the paper with a cup of coffee in his hand. In a shorty robe. That would make my Christmas. That would make my goddamn year."

Vince pauses in cutting Jodi's hair so he can laugh. "I'd like to change my answer."

Jodi says, "How would you know where he lives, Darla?"

"My cousin has a police scanner," Darla says. "I know exactly where he lives."

A tin of cookies Louisa baked returns from making a revolution around the salon. Everyone is eating cookies.

Darla nods, approving of the gingersnap in her hand. "I'm writing a novel," she says. "So many people tell me my life would make a great book. I figure I'll give it a shot."

"Like who tells you that?" Vince says.

"Like everyone."

Jodi says, "You should put Louisa in your novel. Ex-dancer who bakes delicious cookies."

Darla considers it. "Louisa would be a good, what do they call it, background character. Not the main one. Main characters are more . . . I don't want to say interesting, but more, dynamic? You can be the main character's friend, Louisa."

Louisa concentrates on the magazine in her lap.

"Maybe I'll put you in my novel, Jodi."

"Give me hair like Louisa's," Jodi says, "and a husband who doesn't speak English."

"I will if I can," Darla says, "but the creative process is tricky. I'm at the mercy of the muse."

"I get that," Jodi says.

2:00 P.M.

Cassidy, the new bartender, sweeps the floor. Cigarettes, dirt, stray earrings, a pick, glimmer in the dustpan. When she told Lorca during their brief interview that she was named after the song, Lorca asked what song, and she rolled her eyes and said, " 'Cassidy'? By the Grateful Dead?"

"I don't know new music," Lorca said.

"It's like forty years old!"

Cassidy lines up stuffed trash bags by the door. Her hair is brick-colored and she has a way of making every word sound like a curse. "You guys set a fire in here last night?"

Lorca passes her a bucket of soapy water and a pile of dry towels. "You start there, I'll start here." He lowers himself onto his knees. The hammering in his shins begins in earnest, but if he supports himself on one fist, he can manage. He plunges the rag into the water and works it over the corner of floor. The heat feels good on his hands. He moves the rag over the unseen parts of the bar, gathering clots of dust and debris. The work satisfies him and he likes that he can see the result, the wood returning to near its original color. He and Cassidy back toward each other until they meet in the center of the room and he can no

78

longer ignore his humming knees. "You got it from here?" He chucks the rag into the pail.

Cassidy surveys the floor and nods, content. "Only way to clean a floor is on your hands and knees," she says.

In the back room, Gray Gus uses a magnifying glass to paint orderly stripes on the wings of his plane. Sonny reads on his cot in the walk-in freezer, slippered feet pulsing to the jazz coming from an old radio. The very day he and the guys returned from Chicago to help Lorca run the club, Sonny claimed the walk-in for his bedroom. He removed the bottom row of shelves to fit his cot and a night table that held a slim pair of reading glasses and whatever he was reading, these days Chekhov's collected stories. Sonny is particular in his solos and in his sock drawer. His pants make prim stacks on the shelves; his shirts line the meat racks on hangers. A Dopp kit of soaps for when he half-showers in the kitchen's industrial sink.

When Lorca enters, Gus looks up, eyes still narrowed in focus. "Can we talk?"

Lorca detects a note of gravity unusual for the easygoing drummer.

"He guessed," Sonny says.

Gus replaces the cap to the bottle of paint and wheels his chair up to Lorca's desk. "I can help," he says. "I have money."

"You have thirty thousand dollars?" Lorca says.

"Jesus." Gus pushes himself away from the desk. "I don't have that much."

Sonny marks the page in his book. "I told you it was a ridiculous amount."

"I thought you meant, like, a couple hundred." Gus brushes excess filings from the plane's body, the remnants from sanding a wing or a door.

"A couple hundred could not be classified as 'ridiculous.'"

"Depends on who you ask," Gus says.

Lorca leaves them to debate. He hoists two trash bags from the line and carries them outside. By the Dumpster, a dog the size of a standard amp wrestles a milk carton.

"Dog," he says. "Come here."

The dog abandons the battle and runs over. It throws itself onto the ground to announce its belly. "I know you." Lorca fishes around its neck to find the tag.

Ciao! I'm Pedro.

I have a case of wanderlust.

If found, please call . . .

Cassidy stands behind him holding two more bags. "What's that?" she says. "A dog?"

3:00 P.M.

Already evening is blotting out the city. Shadows web in the alleys on Ninth Street. The illuminated crew houses of Boathouse Row reflect in the unimpressed Schuylkill. The factory near Palmer belches filth toward New Jersey. Clouds flinch across the mackerel sky, bottoms silvered by the retreating sun.

Vince and Darla smoke in front of Beauty Land while inside, Jodi throws the switch. The sign ignites in pink and gold bulbs. "Should we sing?" Darla says.

Lorca walks Pedro down South Street, a lightweight rope improvised for a leash, grateful for the errand. There is a phone call he needs to make in private. Even on citation-less days, Sonny has a preternatural interest in Lorca's schedule, but the cop's visit has triggered the full breadth of his anxiety. *Where are you going? When will you be back?* Sonny asked three times before Lorca left.

Pedro jockeys sideways, hoping to trick the leash off. He tries contrary directions. He darts through parted legs, leaving Lorca to apologize around the last-minute shoppers. At a *Don't Walk* light, the dog whines, pleads.

"You're not the only one trying to escape."

Lorca points to a cedar-colored Rottweiler across the street, also trying to rid itself of a leash while its owner is distracted on a phone call. The collar slips off after another thrust and the dog freezes, stunned by success. Then, as if realizing the temporary nature of its fortune, the dog unlocks and gallops down South Street. Muscles beaming, it cuts such a figure that Lorca forgets what he's watching is dangerous. A little girl points mutely. "That dog is running," she reports to her mother. The Rottweiler's agenda is a pit bull puppy waiting at a corner with its owner. Before Lorca can cross, because by now he, Pedro, and the rest of the street have realized the impending danger, the Rottweiler clamps onto the puppy's neck and lifts it over the holiday scene.

The pit bull's owner blinks at the two-canine altercation, unable to speak. The Rottweiler thrashes the puppy with elation. Its owner arrives, bringing new information, that the dog is a she, and her name is—"Grace!" she says. "Drop it." A police officer is urged through the crowd by worried shoppers. He raises his gun, which has the desired effect of widening his working circle.

Lorca becomes light-headed. He can't get clear which dogs are fighting and which are trying to take his club. The dogs in the fight. The dog by his side. The cop with a gun. The cop at the door. These dogs will be okay, he thinks, because they are not real. He is some way making this happen.

Isn't he? These aren't real onlookers. That isn't real blood. They will find the money. He won't lose his club. Louisa will get over whatever mortal sin he committed and call him back. Suddenly, he feels hopeful, helpful.

"You can't pull a dog from a dog," he offers.

"I know that," the officer says. "Don't you think I know that?" He fires a nervous shot into the sky. Someone near Lorca screams. The Rottweiler drops the puppy, which takes a few foggy steps before being collected by its owner.

The officer replaces his gun in the holster. "Yes," he says to the puppy being tended by its owner. "Yes," he says to the Rottweiler being recollared. "Yes," he says to the sky where he deposited the bullet. He bats at perspiration on his neck. He is coming to terms. "I wasn't sure for a second, guys," he says. "But that will just about do it."

3:05 P.M.

Alex Lorca uses his key to let himself into his father's apartment. The oniony smell of old drapes and carpet. The mail heaped against the door. In the bedroom's honeyed light, Louisa folds clothes into suitcases. "You scared me," she says, not looking scared. "I forgot you have a lesson."

Alex perches in the doorway. "You colored your hair."

"It's too much." She swats at it. "Do you think so?"

"It's beautiful." His voice is flat, unbiased. "You're leaving."

"What happened to my geranium?" She points to a weary plant on the sill. "It was healthy and strong three days ago. I told your father, don't forget to water her. The one thing I asked. There's no talking to that man." She crosses to Alex and takes his chin in her hand. The immediacy of her never fails to please him. He can tell she's been crying, but Louisa's expression is always that of someone looking at some meaningful, tragic thing. Even when she's chewing out a distributor for overcharging them. Even when she's looking at him. "I'm leaving," she says.

"That fat jag made you leave."

84

"Don't call your father names. One day he'll be dead."

"One day we'll all be dead," Alex says.

"Him first, though, because he eats like a farm animal."

Alex doesn't smile. He feels his life fast-forwarding, *thwip-thwipping* quicker than he can handle. "Where are you going?" he says.

"My brother's for now. When I find a place, I'll have a key made for you so you can crash when you come in from your mother's house, instead of here. This place isn't healthy. Nothing can grow." She zips the suitcases. "Least of all future famous guitarists."

Alex fidgets in the doorway. He doesn't know what to do when she speaks like this. She is always telling him to watch his hands, or bringing home brochures from the city's best music schools. But how would he ever get his father to approve? Lorca's rule is no guitar. No matter how much Alex or Louisa pleads. From age six, however, Sonny and the guys had sneaked lessons whenever Lorca was at the club. Sometimes it was Sonny, sometimes Max, depending on who could get away. The last place Lorca would ever suspect, his own apartment.

Alex carries the suitcases. Louisa scoops up the plant and follows him into the main room.

"You and I," she says, "are always going to be family."

"Family," he spits.

"Kid." She only uses this word when she wants to remind him that she is older and, at least for another year, taller. "We'll still talk every day. I'm still coming to hear you play tonight."

"He won't let me," Alex says. "He said things changed."

"That fat jag." She slumps into a chair. "He's blaming you for me. I'll talk to him."

"There's no talking to that man," he says.

A sound at the door startles them. Sonny enters the kitchen, holding the Snakehead guitar. "Louisa," he says. "What a fun surprise. Haven't seen you around."

"I'm not here to disrupt your lesson," she says. "Good to see you, Sonny."

Sonny registers the suitcases. "Anything you want to talk about?"

She halts in the doorway. "I'd like to talk about why Lorca isn't letting Alex play tonight."

A bead of perspiration wends down Sonny's forehead. "Things changed."

"What changed?"

"Is that a geranium?" Sonny says. "They need indirect sunlight. Otherwise they get ashy."

"Sonny."

"I'm not at liberty to discuss club business, Louisa. He'll kill me."

"On second thought"—Louisa releases the suit-cases with two sharp slaps against the linoleum—

"maybe I'll stay. You guys want eggs? Sonny? You love omelets."

"I could go for some eggs," Alex says.

"You guys will practice," Louisa says. "And I will make eggs. And then, we'll have a nice chat."

"This is entrapment," Sonny says. "I'm being entrapped."

"If you feel trapped, Sonny," Louisa gives Alex a barely perceptible wink, "it's probably because you are."

3:30 P.M.

Madeleine careens through the Ninth Street Market, pulse tremoring.

Her city has a jazz club and it is called The Cat's Pajamas and why hasn't she ever heard of it and how can she get there? It is as if everyone in her life has conspired to hide this from her. Now the only thing that matters is that Madeleine finds it, soon.

This is what Madeleine does not notice because she is distracted: the spice shop's jars of marzipan, kookaburra, Chinese five-spice, mace and coriander, the punching bags of provolone hanging at the cheese shop, the extended yowls of the dried stock fish, hanging in bunches of dead. Normally Madeleine would yowl back at them but she is replaying exactly what they said about The Cat's Pajamas, so she is too busy to notice the crates of pecans pinned by brass shovels, two pounds for five dollars, the curling snakes of apple sausages, dollar-a-bag candy, gossiping vendors, so and so, and so and so. Madeleine passes the barrels of fire, the grocer weighing spinach on a tipsy scale. She accelerates at the store with the ducks, meadow green avocados, a bluster of brooms, a fire hydrant, the pears, more ducks, she is running, statues, soda, birds, nuts, she turns into Santiago's alley, upsetting a cart of Virgin Mary statuettes. She keeps running, toward the blue carousel horse to whom she forgets to say a proper hello. Madeleine wrests open the café's door to come face to Harlequin romance with Sandra Frankford who has been, for the previous hour, blocking the entrance with the enormous brass flanks of her wheelchair. She grabs hold of Madeleine's wrist.

"Slow it down."

Mrs. Santiago sets the table for lunch. "Look who's back." By the counter, tied to a wine barrel, Pedro sulks. "Jack Lorca found him in Fishtown. Fishtown! That's half a city away. Until he can control his wandering, it's a leash for him."

"I need to use the phone!" Madeleine says.

"Eat your lunch, then you can do whatever you want," Mrs. Santiago says. Then, to Pedro: "No more people food. No more wandering."

Madeleine sits. Sandra can't do anything but sit. Mrs. Santiago sets out plates and silverware and a platter of meats and cheeses. She sits.

"What is The Cat's Pajamas?" Madeleine says.

Sandra bows her head. "Let us pray."

"Amen." Mrs. Santiago hands a basket of bread to Madeleine.

"What is The Cat's Pajamas?" Madeleine says.

Mrs. Santiago stirs sugar into an espresso and watches Pedro, who sniffs the canine food in his bowl. "The Cat's what?"

"Pajamas."

"It's the club Jack Lorca owns. Pedro was eating from the trash like a criminal!"

"I heard a report yesterday"—Sandra butters a piece of bread—"about a man in London who made a three-bedroom house out of trash."

Pedro gives the food a suspicious lick. Mrs. Santiago bites her thumbnail. "He doesn't like it."

"Where is it? Can anyone go?" Madeleine says.

"It's near Ireland," says Sandra. "Of course anyone can go."

"You're not going to London," Mrs. Santiago says. "Yummy, Pedro." She rubs her stomach. "Good food."

"Not London," Madeleine says. "The Cat's Pajamas."

"A jazz club is no place for a little girl," Mrs. Santiago says. "Stop swinging your legs."

Madeleine stops swinging. "I want to go."

Mrs. Santiago waves her hand as if shooing a fly. "I want to ride in a hot-air balloon. Hover over the city like a bird would."

"I don't know how that relates to me," Madeleine says.

"Like this: Me is to hot-air balloon as you is to The Cat's Pajamas. Neither is going to happen!"

"We'll see about that."

Mrs. Santiago raises herself up to her full height: five foot two in kitchen clogs. She wipes each hand on her calico apron and regards Madeleine with a patient gaze.

"Madeleine," she says. "There are roaches at The Cat's Pajamas. Mean, fist-sized roaches that drink alcohol and latch onto the necks of little girls. They turn all the lights out because no one there is afraid of the dark and they laugh at people who are. The Cat's Pajamas is a meeting place for gypsies who eat roaches. Gypsies, roaches, and ice cream men."

At nine, Madeleine is only approaching the summit of understanding that sometimes adults lie to get what they want. "Ice cream men?" she tests.

"Like the ice cream man with the cleft lip who scares you so much when he rings his bell down Ninth Street."

"Why would anyone go there if it was so horrible?" she says.

"People are strange." Mrs. Santiago sips her espresso. "But I do have a surprise for you." She reveals a box from underneath the table. Inside pose several shiny hats. She places one on her head and adjusts its rubber tie around her chin. It is blue with streamers exploding from the top.

"Won't your friends love these when they come to your party?"

Madeleine excuses herself and escapes into the back room, where everything is bleached senseless. In the yellow pages she locates the listing for The Cat's Pajamas. Even the name on the page excites her. She runs her fingers over it. It is a place that exists and has a listing in the phone book and it is not in a distant city, it is here, in hers. She dials.

On the first ring, an accented voice croons, "You have reached The Cat's Pajamas. I am the owner. How may I be of service?"

Behind him, intoxicating, electric nothing.

"Hello?" the man says. Then, in a lower, more intimate tone. "Is this a ghost?"

Madeleine hears several throaty guffaws and hangs up. Richmond Street, Fishtown. If she walks north she will hit South Street, which belts the city. If she takes South all the way to the river, the numbers will recede. If she turns up Second she will eventually get to Fishtown. She's never been that far. If she wears sneakers and walks fast, she can get there in—

"Madeleine!" Sandra raps against the arm of her wheelchair. "Time to read!"

Madeleine returns to the front room, where Sandra holds a slim volume titled *The Edge of Beyond*. On the cover, a woman in a safari hat glares into the beyond. Behind her, a man in sunglasses leers.

Sandra ahems, removes her sunset-colored bifocals, and closes her eyes—her prereading ritual. "Page thirty-five."

Madeleine reads. When she encounters a thorn in pronunciation, normally a vowel-consonant blend, she holds out the book to Sandra, who replaces her glasses, then announces it in her rude baritone.

". . . Every time she thought of the way he had kissed her, she shook in—"

"Inwardly!" shouts Sandra, summoning Pedro from a nap.

". . . Of course she hadn't wanted it; she had done her very best to free herself from his—"

"Restraining embrace!"

"She tried to think of something else, anything else, so she didn't have to admit the . . ."

"Humiliating truth!"

". . . Humiliating truth to herself that in the end she hadn't resisted him at all. She had clung to him like a drowning man seeking the breath of life."

Sandra clucks. "Poor, misguided Rosalind."

They trudge through chapters six and seven. Madeleine yearns to get outside. Pedro saunters by, inquiring about her ankle.

A word about Pedro.

Who keeps his salt-and-pepper hair in a state of managed chaos, jutting out from four nimble legs and hindquarters, muscular from distance walking. Whose brown eyes hold the world-weariness characteristic of a bon vivant. Who is enough Yorkshire terrier to exhibit daffy wonderment, and enough Welsh Scottie to accomplish a goal with focus. Pedro hops up on his hind legs in an effort to secure the candy Mrs. Santiago is currently figure-eighting over his snout. She takes too long to relent so when she does, Pedro respectfully declines. He is a gentleman wanderer who yearns to explore. Madeleine yearns for an exit. Rosalind yearns for a lover.

A blond head with pigtails approaches the store. Jill McCormick enters, in a clatter of bells. Seeing Madeleine, she narrows her eyes. "Did you get your hair cut? You missed lab."

Madeleine checks to see if Mrs. Santiago is listening. "I was there but you didn't see me."

"My eye doctor said these glasses give me better than twenty-twenty vision." Jill is a practical literalist. On hot days when Saint Anthony's is too broke to turn on the air-conditioning, the kids fold paper into fans. Jill likes to point out: you expend more energy fanning yourself than you do just sitting there.

"Can you see this?" Madeleine says.

"You're sticking up your middle finger."

Mrs. Santiago calls hello from behind the counter.

"Hello," Jill says. "I've come for a pound of coffee for my mom. The Sumatran. She wants to branch out."

Mrs. Santiago winks at the portrait of her late husband. "Daniel's favorite!"

"Who's Daniel?" says Jill. "Oh. Your dead husband."

A plan forms in Madeleine's mind. "What are you doing today?" she says.

Jill stiffens. "I'm organizing my stuffed animals into color order and then I'm reorganizing them into size order, why?"

"Can I come over?"

Jill peers at her through her thick glasses. "Are you good at organizing?"

"Who will read to me?" Sandra says.

"I'll read to you, dear." Mrs. Santiago hands Jill a brown bag of coffee stamped with Daniel's likeness. As Madeleine expected, she is delighted that she wants to play with another little girl. She comes out from behind the counter holding a leash, on the end of which is a miserable Pedro. "Take him with you. At least he can see some of the outside."

"Pedro seems blue," Jill says.

Mrs. Santiago nods. "His heart is broken."

Pedro backpedals and about-faces, snapping at the leash. Mrs. Santiago asks Pedro what he thinks of a nice walk through the market, a nice walker-oo, wouldn't he like that, a walkcroni roo?

Sandra says, "Why don't you marry that dog?"

Madeleine giggles, in spite of herself. Sandra laughs, too. It takes them several minutes to get themselves under control as Mrs. Santiago waits, unsmiling. Sandra dabs tears from her eyes with a napkin.

"Are you finished?" Mrs. Santiago says.

Madeleine says, "Let's go, Jill."

"Don't forget to ask Jill to come to your birthday par—"

Madeleine slams the door.

"You know who should go to London," Sandra says. "You. You've never been anywhere."

"With all of my spare time." Mrs. Santiago hoots. "Now that's funny."

Outside, Jill asks Madeleine why she will hang out with her all of a sudden. "Did you want to get away from that crazy lady? One of my aunts forces me to read the Bible to her while I comb her hair."

"That's weird," says Madeleine.

"Do you live at Santiago's?"

"I live on Ninth Street in the market with my father."

"Where's your mother?" Jill slaps her forehead. "Oh right! She's dead."

"This is where I leave you," Madeleine says.

Jill blinks several times. "I thought you were coming over."

Madeleine is already legging down the street. "Later skater," she calls over her shoulder.

"You're just mean!" Jill calls to her retreating figure.

Madeleine extends her middle finger above her as she and Pedro gallop toward home.

4:00 P.M.

*O*utside the Red Lion Diner, a girl wearing an expedition coat and pajama bottoms yells into her cell phone that he'd better be coming to pick her up, not whenever he feels like it, but right the hell now.

The lobby no longer has arcade games, but it does have a pay phone. Lorca punches in the number. He holds a plastic container of sausage Mrs. Santiago gave him in thanks for returning her dog. The pajama-ed girl paces outside the window where Lorca stands, listening to the line ring. She wants the person on the other end to explain exactly what kind of asshole he thinks she is. She speaks with the matter-of-fact cruelty of a Northeast girl. They're making young people younger. Or else Lorca is older than he's ever been.

Fiinally, a woman picks up. "Mongoose's."

"I'd like to speak with Mongoose."

"He's not here. May I ask who's calling?"

"When will he be back?"

"He went up the street for sandwiches." The voice inhales sharply. "Lorca? Is that you?"

"Yeah." Lorca closes his eyes. "It's me."

Her tone changes to repentant. "Lorca? How are you?"

97

"I've been better."

"He'll be happy you called," she says. "I'll tell him as soon as he's back. Take care of yourself, Lorca."

He hangs up. The sudden, quiet lobby. The walls are blue with deep yellow flecks. Lorca smells syrup and weak coffee. Inside the glass doors, families sit at plastic booths eating eggs. A waitress borrows a ketchup bottle from one table to give to a family whose food has just arrived.

There he is five years ago, untattooed, fiddling with the knobs of the booth's personal jukebox. It is his first date with Louisa Vicino, snake girl at The Courtland Avenue Club, and he had to bring Alex because the kid threw a tantrum. Louisa doesn't seem to mind. It is going well. In the car ride over, she and Alex discovered they both like Ray Charles and Swiss cheese with no holes.

"When they say vanilla shake"—Louisa studies the menu—"do they mean French or bean? I like bean but not French."

"Me too." Eleven-year-old Alex readjusts himself on the plastic seat so he can sit higher. Lorca is certain his son doesn't know the difference between the two kinds of vanilla. Alex detests Lorca because he won't let him play guitar, but detests being without him even more. Louisa is the first woman his father has allowed him to meet, albeit by force. She is an extension of his father ungoverned by obligatory

98

familial resentment. Alex is free to be fascinated by this full-hipped woman who carries a purse the size of a fist and who declared in the car, "Anyone who doesn't think Ray Charles is the best is a chump."

They order milkshakes. Lorca wants to play Ray Charles on their personal jukebox, but it is broken. Sweat blooms in the fabric of the only button-down he owns.

The Courtland Avenue Club is a combination strip club/bowling alley, a glowing, neon dome you can see from the highway. Louisa dances three times a night and works shifts at the bar in between. Lorca has never seen her dance, and doesn't want to. Her mouth is still red from the outside cold. Lorca likes how her chin moves when she is emphatic. "I didn't finish college," she says, "but I want to take classes. In what I'm not sure."

The milkshakes arrive. She swallows a strawful, then turns to Alex. "How is it?"

He thinks about it. "Good."

"Mine too. If you can flip a spoonful of it over and it doesn't drip, it's good."

A tray of food arrives for the family next to them. The waitress slides each plate onto the table as the family oohs and aahs.

"I have to go to the bathroom," Alex says.

"Hurry up," Lorca says. "We have to get back to the club."

Alex runs off. Louisa stacks a pile of creamers. "You're rough with him."

"I'm real with him. He'll grow up knowing what's real."

"Or he'll grow up hating you."

Lorca feels the day falling off a cliff. "So," he says, "how does someone get into the snake lady business?"

She allows him to change the subject but registers it with a tilt of her pretty eyebrows. "The original snake lady is a friend of mine. We were dancers together, legitimate dancers, in a burlesque show. She said it would be easy money. She was right."

"How do you get them to stay on you?"

"Practice," she says. "I hold my arms in the tank and they wind around." She pantomimes holding her arms in a tank. "When I come onstage, the snakes' heads are down by my hands. I shimmy around, show them to the boys." She sways in the booth to demonstrate. "Then, I go like this." She gyrates on the diner seat. Lorca's neck warms. "They crawl around my belly and legs. I do splits, shimmies, the whole shebang. The snakes are pros. They're the stars and they know it."

"The whole shebang." Lorca is getting a sad feeling. "Do you mix it up every time?"

"I do not," she says, "mix it up."

"What kind of future is in snake dancing?"

"It supported my friend for years," she says. "She's quitting because she has cancer and she wants to be with her kid, but if she didn't, she could have done it indefinitely." She reacts to his grimace. "I like it, Lorca. It's fun."

"Fun," he says. "Do the snakes have names?"

"They have names." She seems less willing to share their names than to talk about the dancing.

"Give."

"Don't laugh," she says. "Hero and Leander. Like the Greek myth?"

"I know like the Greek myth."

Alex returns from the bathroom and asks his father to win him a prize from the claw machine in the lobby. They slip into their coats. Every other table's jukebox works. They walk through several eras of rock and roll, each table its own sad painting: the church crowd, a family, a couple, an old man eating alone. Lorca hears Alex call out the tunes. " 'Fill Me Up, Buttercup,' 'The Twist,' 'God Only Knows,' 'Chances Are.' " Louisa sings along, her voice Marlboro and terrible.

At the register, Lorca waits to pay while Louisa and Alex examine the pie cases. "Coconut custard," she says. "You ever have that?"

Alex wrinkles his nose. "Bleh."

"That's how I feel about it, too. What about that one, Black Forest? I'm a chocolate girl."

Alex's voice is sober. "I'm a chocolate girl, too."

She tousles his thick curls. Alex tries to hide how happy this makes him.

A gleaming bank of machines in the lobby promises prizes in exchange for skill. Alex points to what he wants: a stuffed owl. Lorca feeds a quarter into the machine and nothing happens.

"Two quarters, Dad."

He feeds another quarter. "This only took one when I was a kid."

Louisa says, "Tell it to your plants, old man."

The claw, activated, lurches over the pile of toys. Before Lorca can figure out the buttons, it takes a directionless swipe and misses. The machine shudders to a halt. Lorca feeds it two more quarters.

The claw jerks to life again. This time he is able to position it over the owl. He lowers the claw; its metal hooks close over the animal but drops it when it ascends.

"You suck at this," Louisa says.

Again he feeds the machine two quarters. Again the claw holds the owl for a moment, then drops it. "Is this fixed?" he says. Alex avoids his eyes.

Lorca has one quarter left. He asks Alex for another one. The boy digs through his pockets. "Well?"

"Jesus." Louisa tosses him a quarter from her purse. Lorca tries again. Another failure. He shoves a dollar bill into Alex's hands and tells him to get it changed behind the counter. "Do you want

102

the toy or not?" he says, when the boy hesitates. He turns back to the machine. "They want you to lose all of your money in this thing."

"It's not a big deal," Louisa says, shifting in her heels.

Alex returns with the change. Lorca loses the dollar in less than a minute. On the second attempt, the claw snatches the owl by its wing but at the last second, releases it.

Lorca elbows through the crowd that waits for available tables in thick coats and stockings. The pies in the case shine. He reaches the cashier. "Can someone talk to me about the machine in the lobby? How can I get my son the owl he wants?"

"One minute," says the cashier.

"I'll pay you for one," Lorca says. "I can't spend all day playing a game."

The cashier's smile is thin with aggravation. "It doesn't work that way."

"How about it works that way today?"

The manager is there, asking how he can help. "Why is everything in this place broken?" Lorca says. He leads the man to the lobby, where Louisa and Alex stand by the machine. Alex holds up the stuffed owl. "Louisa got it."

"Lucky, I guess," she says.

Louisa Maya Vicino. Louisa from her Italian grandmother, Maya from her Spanish mother, and Vicino which means "near," because her distant ancestors lived in the vicinity of something important, like an olive grove.

Two weeks later, Lorca's father, Francis, pauses in the middle of a story to readjust his grip on the pilsner he fills. When his head hits the ground, it makes a metallic sound Lorca can hear from the other end of the bar. His father is already dead by the time Lorca reaches him, beer unspooling around him, eyes fixed on some fascination under the bar. Lorca gathers him in his arms.

Gathers him in his name—Jack Francis Lorca.

We carry our ancestors in our names and sometimes we carry our ancestors through the sliding doors of emergency rooms and either way they are heavy, either way we can't escape.

5:00 P.M.

Sarina tries a barrette on her dark hair. She tries the expression she will use when she sees Ben Allen for the first time in four years. Surprise tippling the sides of her mouth. She runs perfume along her collarbone. Getting ready is a series of negotiations with herself and her meager set of prettying items. She settles on a black skirt, champagne blouse, no barrette. She won't do much walking tonight so she makes one final bargain with herself: heels in exchange for a cab ride there.

Thinking about him requires so little effort that she can do it while performing mindless activities. Soaping the dishes, replaiting Clare Kelly's hair, drying the dishes. The part of her brain that plays his ongoing reel is unconnected to the neurons and synapses that control things like conscious thought and logic. Ben turning to her at a party. Ben turning to her. Ben turning. What human being deserves to be the nucleus of such high esteem? Certainly not Benjamin, middle name Hal, last name Allen. Five-nine in boots. Who has a car that doesn't start on cold mornings, an unfinished screenplay, a law degree he doesn't use, a romantic's tendency to save movie stubs, and a mannered, unsmiling wife.

5:15 P.M.

Do you want the good news or the bad news?"
The trash bags are gone, the bar wiped
clean. The lights have been hung; they line the
stage and loop around the Snakehead, making
the old axe glow. Stalled in the doorway, Lorca
experiences a stomachache he can only call
Christmas.

Sonny leans against the bar, arms crossed. "The
good news," he says, "is that Christmas has come
to The Cat's Pajamas. It's like a holiday card in
here. Cassidy hung them. The mouth on that one.
I sent her to get dinner before we open."

"The bad news?"

"We've lost track of Max. He was here, now
he's not. He's not at his place and he's not
answering his phone."

"Do you understand that he is the bandleader
of the Cubanistas?"

"Do I? I do."

"Does he understand that we can't have the
Cubanistas play when the lead Cubanista is not
here?"

"Like I said, he won't answer his phone but
when he does, I will certainly ask him. Did you
call your uncle?"

"I did."

"And?"

"No. But I thought of another option."

"I'm all ears."

"We could sell the Snakehead."

Sonny's hand instinctively moves to protect the guitar hanging over the bar. "Not an option."

"If we want to keep the bar, we have to make sacrifices."

"Your father would roll in his grave," Sonny says.

Lorca pulls on the beer and stares at the guitar. The S-holes, dashing mustaches. The neck and body the color of syrup.

"Who would even buy it, Lorc? Who has that kind of money, or loves guitars that much?"

Lorca doesn't answer.

"There is one more update," Sonny says. "And I don't know if this is good news or bad news. I say it's good news, with bad aspects. Louisa's in the back."

"Why would that be bad news?" Lorca halts in the doorway. "You didn't tell her."

"She guessed!"

In the back room, Louisa sorts through a box of paperwork. She is always more petite than he remembers. For a moment, he lets himself believe he is still her boyfriend and they are having one of their Sunday night disagreements.

"Is he ever going to clean that up?" she says, gesturing to Gus's half-constructed plane.

"He's making progress," Lorca says.

"What's this?" She holds up the citation, the color of prison jumpsuits.

"Something I'm taking care of."

"I'm not here to lecture you. I'm here to get my check and leave."

"It's good to see you, Louisa. I've left a few messages for you. You get any of them?"

"Is my hair different from the last time you saw me?"

Lorca's throat goes dry.

"I cut it," she says. "And dyed it."

"I'm not perceptive, Lou. We know this."

"I'm a minor character in my own life." Her eyes fill. Lorca thinks he will go to her, put his arm around her, but he doesn't move. She waits for his reaction and gets none. Her gaze sharpens. "Alex told me you won't let him play."

"I'll lose my club if he plays."

"He's going down a bad road," she says. "You're choosing not to see it."

The desk phone rings.

Louisa selects her paycheck from the stack and slams the folder shut. "Good-bye!" She disappears into the hallway. "Best of luck!"

"Lou. Wait." He picks up the phone. "Hello."

Someone on the other end clears his throat. "Lorca, it's Mongoose."

"Hang on." Lorca covers the receiver. "Louisa!" He hears her wish Sonny a merry Christmas.

"Come on!" The heavy thud of the front door closing. He leaves the phone on the desk. The hallway is dark and long and empty. "Louisa?" His voice echoes against the walls as if he is asking himself her name.

6:00 P.M.

Madeleine unlayers by the door to her apartment. The day's dressing and undressing has exhausted her. She unleashes Pedro, who conducts a cursory study of every bookshelf base and table leg.

In the bathroom the toilet wails: Clare! Claaaarrrrrre!

Madeleine has learned to pre-announce her arrival in rooms to give the roaches time to scatter. "I am in the family room!" she cries. "I am walking from the family room to the bathroom!"

She switches on the bathroom light and closes her eyes for three beats. She lifts the back lid off the toilet, uses the watering can to fill the basin, then replaces the lid. The toilet quiets.

"I am walking from the bathroom to the kitchen!"

In the kitchen, she fills a bowl of water for Pedro and turns the kettle on.

The voice of Nina Simone drifts in from her father's bedroom, remorseless as cigarette smoke. It grows louder. Madeleine's father will adjust the volume ten to fifteen times during a song, sitting in arm's distance of the player, surrounded by his library of vinyl and books. There are three record players in the apartment and no milk. One of her father's jazz books would have an

110

entry on The Cat's Pajamas. Why hadn't she thought of this? She could sneak in there, but she must be quiet, like cancer. Madeleine's father insists on silence. Except for bringing his meals, she doesn't disturb him.

She opens his door and breathes in: pecorino, Havarti. His mussed bed near the window. He dozes on one of two camel-colored chairs in the center of the room, clasping each arm as if in sleep he might take off. His chin rests on the collar of his satiny sweater. By his elbow, a tube of pills. It is possible he changed the record in a dream. Every day the line between his reality and sleep blurs more. Every day more roaches.

Madeleine sees the book she needs: *History of Jazz, Volume Two*. She tiptoes across the room and coaxes it from its place on the bookshelf. Nina Simone goes on singing, unaffected.

Black is the color of my true love's hair.

The record skips.

Black is the color
Black is the color

Madeleine lunges toward the record to move the needle but miscalculates the distance. Nina Simone yelps. Her father stirs, issuing a blubbery command.

The color
The color

Madeleine fixes the needle too late. Her father's eyes launch open.

Who is this girl, Mark Altimari wonders, flapping big eyes at him? He bats at the coffee table for his glasses and secures them over his ears with shaky hands. His daughter comes into focus.

"Madeleine." His expression sweetens. "Where have you been?"

"In the other room."

He invites her to sit in the other chair. The song changes to a faster one. Nina Simone says there's a lot of trouble with a brown-eyed handsome man. "Have you heard this one before?"

Madeleine nods.

"Can you hear it? Should I raise the volume?"

"I can hear it."

"You'd like this recording. It has your singers and your stand-up bass. Wonderful stand-up bass player . . . I don't remember his name."

Music fills the space between them. Mark wants to take the pill that keeps him awake, but not in front of his daughter. Instead, he flirts. "There's a lot of trouble with a brown-eyed handsome man. In your travels have you found this to be true?"

This is Madeleine's favorite game. His role is

to ask silly questions and hers is to answer as if he is serious, neither one acknowledging the other conversation that goes on wordlessly around them, in which some other, better version of themselves say: Isn't it nice to be father and daughter?

"Oh yes," Madeleine says. "Once I lost both my arms in a wrestling match to meet a brown-eyed handsome man."

"That is a lot of trouble!" He folds his hands, pleased. "Are you enjoying school?"

"Yes," she fibs.

"Good. It's in your blood, you know."

"What's in my blood, Dad?" Madeleine speaks carefully, not wishing to disturb the tenuous crochet between them. She does not swing her legs.

"All of it, dear."

The teapot's whistle barges in from the other room.

Madeleine hops off the chair. "It's my tea. I'll take it off the stove." She opens the door and Pedro pounces in.

Her father's eyebrows jolt toward the ceiling. "What is that?"

Madeleine calls Pedro back into the other room but he ignores her, sniffing the legs of her father's chair. Pedro has had a rough day that involved, among other things, incarceration via leash. He wants to bound and spring and hope and the time is now. He leaps onto a bookcase shelf but finds no solid ground. He pedals against a stack of comic books. Dog and shelf crash unceremoniously down, narrowly missing Madeleine's father. A journal catapults, tizzying the record needle.

There's a lot of trouble with a brown-eyed handsome man
Brown-eyed handsome man

Madeleine's father shrieks, atonal with fear. She debates whether to go after the record or Pedro or the teapot. Her father picks up an alarm clock and throws. It hits Pedro on his side. The dog squeaks in pain and leaps through the open window.

"Pedro! No!" Madeleine runs to the window in time to see the dog bound past the Dumpsters toward the twinkling of Ninth Street.

Her father is standing. He palms the swell of her neck and pins her against a bookshelf. His cheeks tremble. His eyes, shot through with blue, are focused on some unseen slight. Madeleine can smell his hand lotion, anisette and vetiver. His thumb presses into her windpipe and she begins to choke. She clasps onto his elbow, as if to help him.

"Dad," she says, to remind him that she is his daughter.

He blinks, clearing whatever spell has him. He

releases her and sits on the chair, in shock. He begins to cry. Madeleine darts to the kitchen and slaps off the burner underneath the teapot, which pitches and empties its water onto the stove. It takes her years to wrench the front door open. Her father's bellowing gains velocity and chases her down the hallway. She runs behind the building, but the dog is gone.

Back in the apartment, the sound has ceased. Her father has retreated into his bedroom and locked the door. Madeleine pours a cup of tea and calls Mrs. Santiago, who immediately becomes overwrought and hangs up. Two roaches charge down the kitchen wall in a race they abandon halfway through. They idle.

Madeleine stares through the window into the courtyard. On most days she feels something staring back: a God or a mother-shaped benevolent force. Today, nothing reciprocates. The streamers on the chained bicycles lift in the indifferent breeze. She is alone in old stockings she's repaired twice but still run. Life will be nothing but errands and gray nights.

Madeleine cries. Cries more when she asks herself what she could be doing while the tea is brewing, more when she fastens the clothespin onto her nose, more when she remembers the word *ungrateful,* more when she thinks of the caramel apples. She longs to hear her mother's voice: a round, dulcet sound, ridged with spice.

Madeleine pities her classmates, whose mothers' voices are wry or weak, eliciting no allegiance from family members or vendors no matter how loud they yell. Madeleine's mother was, at her quietest, her most powerful. Her voice could reverse the terms of every unfair transaction.

She thumbs through her mother's recipe box for anything that will help: HOW TO SEW A BUTTON, HOW TO MAKE WRAPPING RIBBON INTO CURLICUES, HOW TO CHECK CAR OIL, HOW TO TALK ABOUT A BOOK YOU HAVEN'T READ.

Finally, she finds:

HOW TO GET OVER THE POETIC HORRORS.
Ice cream
Chocolate
Whiskey
Nina Simone, "Live at the Village Gate"
Dance
National Geographic
Get your hair and nails done
Sing

Madeleine brings her tea to the mirror where a girl with a freshly bowled haircut stares back. All she sees is nose. She adjusts the clothespin. She selects a record and waits for the song to begin.

Hey there, you with the stars in your eyes.

It is impossible to be sad when she is singing, even if the song she's singing is sad. She marks "You with the Stars in Your Eyes" down in her notes. C minus.

She wants to keep practicing, but she is tired. Pedro is loose in the city. Her father is fastened to his room, with his records and his drugs and his quiet. She crawls under her covers. It is her fault for triggering one of his spells. At least it had been brief. She knows most girls do not have to deal with a father like hers. Most girls would be scared of his fits, and the way she lives, lawless in a roachy apartment. Madeleine would be scared too, she thinks, falling asleep. If she had only experienced finished basements and dads who acted like dads. But Madeleine loves her father, and how can you be scared of someone you love?

6:30 P.M.

Sarina chooses a bottle of wine for the party at the corner store. Tinsel glints on the door and windows. The tree in the produce aisle revolves on its pedestal, reflecting red and silver light onto whoever buys grapes. "Surfer Girl" plays on the overhead speakers and everyone Sarina passes in the aisles is singing.

6:40 P.M.

*G*ood-bye, children, good-bye. Tucked into your buses, secured into the hands of your parents or guardians on the approved list of who can pick you up. Principal Randles walks the halls of Saint Anthony, tapping off lights and shutting doors. Except for the art projects that flutter in her wake, nothing moves. The chalk dust has settled.

In her office, Principal Randles pours a glass of single malt. At home, a sink full of dishes and a poster of Paris at night. On Christmas she will volunteer at the convent, collecting the old nuns' drool with cheap napkins.

What had the Altimari girl said? *Santa doesn't exist,* with the same flip tone her mother, Corrine, had. Like her mother, this girl has no appreciation for a principal's job. Someone has to enforce lines and ring bells and guide and discipline. The way that woman walked, like she was paying the sidewalk a favor. She hadn't believed Corrine would actually die. But what had the girl called her? A bitch rag?

Principal Randles is going on a date tonight with a tax attorney who described himself on his profile as a culinary enthusiast. *Ha-ha,* she says to the empty office. Bitch rag, indeed. She wears a

119

new dress the color of cornflowers and they are going to a restaurant whose patrons eat in plastic, glowing pods. She wants to show off the legs she maintains with Olympian discipline.

Principal Randles stands in the doorway to the main office, mood buoying. She watches her secretary, Regina, count pretzel money, all the hem- ming and hawing parts of her; the unexplained bag of yarn, the Christmas gifts heaped upon her in card, ceramic, and doodad form, the battery-powered vest that exclaims: HAPPY HOLIDAYS! Then goes quiet. HAPPY HOLIDAYS! Then goes quiet. Regina is in teaching for the outfits. By her elbow a pile of erasers waits to be clapped.

"Regina." The principal wags her scotch. "Go home."

"But the erasers."

"Forget them."

The secretary has too many bags, so the principal follows her through the schoolyard to her sagging Nissan. She watches Regina drive out of the parking lot, the reflection of her vest insisting HAPPY HOLIDAYS! against the wind- shield.

A figure crouches near the trees that border the yard.

"Who is that?" she calls.

It is a boy she doesn't recognize. He considers her, then scurries away. She walks to where he had been kneeling. A line of trees dusted with dead leaves. A piece of chalk, a drained soda can, and a phrase written on the asphalt.

BITCH

Mindless graffiti, she assures herself, back-handing a stray tear from her cheek.

6:45 P.M.

*L*orca sits at his desk, stabbing Mrs. Santiago's sausage out of its container with a plastic fork. Mongoose will come in later to buy the Snakehead. The club will be saved, Sonny will roil, spring will come, and maybe by then Lorca will shake the feeling of sliding down a hill of ice that gets steeper as he falls, reaching out for anything substantial but finding ice, and ice, and ice.

Mongoose, the traitor. The desk phone rings. It is Gray Gus, five years earlier, calling to tell Lorca about a girl he's just met.

He, Mongoose, and Sonny had chased a promoter's late-night oath to Chicago. Charlie Roads went with them, a childhood friend of Gus's who was a bookie and a drug dealer.

The promoter sets the boys up with a gig playing The C Note three times a week. Gus meets a girl from the South Side named Alessandra. She writes her name and number on a piece of paper and it takes up the whole page in *A*'s and *S*'s. Everything is that name Alessandra. He rides the El. Alessandra. He buys the paper to check the box scores. Alessandra. The street kids slap playing cards into the spokes of their bike wheels. Al-es-san-dra. He carries her number around for a week before he calls her.

122

Alessandra has ten brothers and sisters. She is a neighborhood girl, a gem. Gus decides she can follow him out of those slums like a star. He calls Lorca late at night from pay phones all around Chicago to say words like *alabaster* and *resplendent,* the relief of her perfect face.

"Are you having a stroke?" Lorca says.

Charlie convinces Gus to take bets on horses. Charlie has a wife and little boy, so Gus gives him the lion's share when they win. Gus doesn't care about money, as long as he has enough for his fix and a pack of cigars to smoke during his gigs at The C Note. But instead of taking care of his family, Charlie places bigger bets with more seasoned dealers. "Reinvesting," he calls it. He loses, and begins to dodge a bookie named Leland.

Gus was born with a Hollywood chin, a butter touch, and an ear that can hear rhythms tapped out from Neptune. In another life he would have been drumming in Johnny Carson's band, drinking water out of a mug. But in this one he has a disease and he can't say no to shysters like Charlie, who uses his wife and kid to cheat on Gus's lousy, glowing heart.

Lorca warns him over the phone, "They're going to break your hands, Gus, and you'll never play again."

In love, Gus is a mess. "They can take my hands," he snorts. "I don't need them."

Alessandra sews a warm lining into his old coat,

salves his arms with cotton balls soaked in crèmes from her sister's salon. She cooks big meals. Gus sends Lorca a picture: him grinning loonily at one end of a table, and her at the other, holding a noodle salad. Between them in dozens of chairs are her brothers and sisters, variations on Alessandra. After dinner, he ties up and they sit on her roof. They put the best views of a city in its worst neighborhoods. She holds him while he pukes.

He says she sings like Patsy Cline. She calls him *lupo grigio*, Gray Wolf.

"When you're not around," she says, "my days are gray."

Leland and his buddies find Gus at The C Note, looking for Charlie. It is late, and Gus isn't feeling any pain. He won't tell them where Charlie is, so they beat him up and take his coat.

They find Mongoose in a corner store. He doesn't run, or take it for his friend. The next morning, a janitor stumbles over Charlie on a train platform, so brained in Gus has to identify him by his sleeve of tattoos at the morgue. Then he goes on a bender, a weeklong disaster. Charlie's debt falls to him, so one night he lets himself into Alessandra's house and creeps into one of the empty upstairs bedrooms. One of the sisters catches him going through her purse and calls for Alessandra. Alessandra isn't mad. She gives him what she has. There's no fight to be had, but Gus fights, anyway. He tells her she is only good for one thing. They scream at each other on the front staircase: Alessandra in tears and Gus so high he won't remember the names he keeps spitting at her until they drag him away.

He stumbles to The C Note and passes out behind the bar. When he wakes up a penny post-card has arrived with news from Lorca.

Francis Lorca is dead. Jack Lorca has inherited The Cat's Pajamas. He is calling everyone home. Bring your guitars, your Alessandras. Come home.

To Gus, clothes papery with dirt, Lorca is offering a place to get quiet. It is as if his future is revealed to him like the archangel coming down to Mary, only this is a crappy postcard, a soft pretzel with arms and legs, dancing on a word spelled out in cartoon letters.

Gus and Sonny move back and join the Cubanistas. Sam Mongoose moves back too and opens his own club in Center City. Lorca ignores his phone calls until he stops calling. Gus goes clean and quiet, and never ties up again. The last time Gus sees Alessandra is through the elbows and arms of her brothers and sisters who force themselves in between them.

That's a drummer's love story. If you want a prettier one, you'll be waiting forever. If you could separate your body into four distinct rhythms, you'd be cracked too.

7:00 P.M.

Jt is dark, dark seven P.M. on Christmas Eve Eve.

The city gathers its black-skirted taxis around the ankles of Rittenhouse Square. A vendor rolls his cart into the park. Pinwheels hem and sigh in flowerpots stuffed with foam. Every audience in every theater on Broad Street leans forward into the hyphen of silence between the overture and Act One. A couple necks in the backseat of a Honda parked at Thirteenth and Spruce.

Ted Stempel leaves for his shift at the store. His battered pit bull puppy, Malcolm, gazes at him. "On second thought," he says to his wife, "I'll take him with me."

Once in a while a gust of evergreen settles over the man selling Christmas trees on Walnut. It really is nice, he thinks, that smell. In Olde City a girl follows her breath down the street, drifting away from her friends. "Look." She claps her mittened hands. "Look!"

Madeleine is sleeping.

On her building's rooftop, Mrs. Santiago unclips a shirt and yanks the laundry line toward her, unclips a bra then yanks, and so forth, until the line has been yanked empty, its contents folded into a wicker basket. She watches the Market-

126

Frankford El slice across the horizon. She's never been on a plane. She wants to take a trip, but she has to fold the laundry. Find the dog. Freeze the gravy. Take care of the child who lately has seemed troubled and distracted.

Mrs. Santiago once cooked for three days in preparation for Christmas, then spent the entire meal running back to the kitchen for a cheese grater, a certain pepper, a record someone mentioned. Borne back ceaselessly into the kitchen.

A faraway ambulance screams through the city.

Mrs. Santiago prays: *Little Flower, show your power at this hour.*

In Georgina McGlynn's kitchen, Sarina uses wooden tongs to refresh a salad. She was the first guest to arrive and now suffers through the aneurysm of the doorbell, heralding another guest, Bella and Claudia and Michael, so far. So far, things are not going well. Her presence has caused glances of confusion (Bella), raised eyebrows (Michael), and one pointed "Who are you, though?" (Claudia). This has made Sarina nervous, resulting in several earnest exclamations regarding the salad. Breathtaking, she called it. More confused glances caused her to call the baked potatoes badass.

The necking couple at Thirteenth and Spruce has fogged up most of the Honda's windows. The man presses his lips against the woman's neck, her earlobe. Her eyes are closed, but she leans forward as if straining to see something through the misted window, Ben Allen perhaps, who is several yards away coaxing the last drag from his cigarette. Ben had been about to leap the stairs to Georgie's house when he caught sight of the pawing couple. He watches until nostalgia forms in his lower gut—he once made slow work of someone's neck, but whose? Certainly not Annie's—but not long enough to be a cad. He takes Georgie's steps in two leaps, as usual the last to arrive. His sanctified role in this group is showing up unforgivably late but armed with a story of what kept him that is so compelling he is at once forgiven. He shakes himself out of his coat in Georgie's entryway. "You will not believe what is happening on your very street, Georgie." He waits until she pauses in her work lighting candles and Bella and Claudia turn, to announce, "A couple is making out in a car."

"Where?" Bella runs to the window. "I want to see."

"There," he points.

"Gross." Georgie waves out a match.

"Not gross, Georgie. Inspiring." He surveys the room—the smell of cinnamon, the sputtering candles, the friends he's had since forever—through the eyes of strangers making out in a Honda. "Doesn't it make you happy to be in the world?"

"Doesn't what make you happy to be in the

world?" Sarina Greene enters the room holding a salad. Ben's coat gets stuck halfway off. It pins him, turns him around. She watches him flail. Finally he wrenches free. "That coat tried to kill me," he says. "You're a witness."

She giggles.

Bella introduces Ben to her new girlfriend, Claudia, who works with crack-addicted war veterans. Claudia tells Ben about her recent obsession with Hitchcock. People with service jobs create a pang of guilt in Ben. When does she have time to watch movies?

"Where is Annie?" Georgie says.

Ben delivers the line he rehearsed. "Home sick, she sends this wine." He produces a bottle of red that Georgie and Sarina inspect. "It's from a town where she spent summers. I'd tell you, but she says I pronounce it wrong."

"How nice." Georgie hands the bottle to Sarina, who it seems has become Assistant to the Dinner. She disappears into the kitchen.

Sarina attended high school with Ben, Georgie, Bella, and Michael but wasn't what they would call "core." She was a misfit in their pasteurized, suburban school. A bright spot, dressed in black. Earlier in the afternoon, when Ben had made the customary do-you-need-anything phone call, Georgie told him Sarina had been invited because of an intersection of location, timing, and pie. Georgie said they had engaged in a dangerous fraction of conversation, marked by perceived insult and overaccommodation: *Would you like to come, sadly no, not that I don't want to, well then you must, well then I absolutely will!*

Michael whispers into Ben's ear. "Did you happen to see my car? Brand-new. Silver. Custom rims."

"Michael has finally come to terms with the fact that he's in finance," Georgie says.

"Didn't see it," Ben says. "Unless it has two people making out in it."

"Two sunroofs," Michael says.

"Two?"

Michael holds up two fingers. "Keeping up with the Joneses and all."

"I see them!" Bella says. She and Michael and Ben and Georgie and Claudia peer out the window.

Georgie's apartment hovers over the corner of Thirteenth and Spruce like a brick exclamation point, between Pine's sleepy antique shops and the tattooed disinterest of South. When she bought it, they toasted her new life: the boutique she was about to open, the marriage. The exclamation then was: the world is kind enough to allow all things! The boutique closed after ten months of vacuuming the carpet early. The marriage ended after five months of fretful sex. The exclamation now is: I am petrified!

"To life." Michael lifts his glass.

To life, the party replies.

Dinner begins. The plate of bread circumnavigates the table. The table is round, so no one sits at the head. Or everyone does, Michael thinks, slicing into the butter. Because it is a good dinner party, food is beside the point. Who cares what Georgie served? Vegetable lasagna and heirloom whatnot. A breathtaking salad.

Sarina taps salt from a reindeer shaker. "Salt," she says, "is a combination of sodium and chloride. They are considered the bad boys of the periodic table. I learned that from our science teacher."

"It is also what you give people who've recently moved into a house," Ben says. "For luck in fertility. Or a seasoned life. One of those."

Claudia gives a clipped ha-ha. "Who can afford a house?"

"I bought a house," Michael says. "But it's more to keep up with the Joneses."

Bella wavers on her choice of bread but commits. "How long have you been back in the city, Sarina?"

"Not even a year."

"Weren't you living someplace fabulous and foreign?" Georgie says.

"Connecticut," Sarina says.

"It's no surprise you're back." Michael spoons potatoes onto his plate. "This city has the highest recidivism rate in America."

"What does that word mean?" Georgie says.

"It means you have no options." Ben salts his salad. "You can't get away, no matter how hard you try."

"Whatever happened to that guy you dated for so long, Sarina?" Bella says, as if the thought has just occurred to her.

"I married him."

"You could have brought him," Georgie pouts. "Where is he tonight?"

Sarina swallows a throatful of greens. "Divorced."

The party flicks their eyes to her, to their plates. Georgie keeps Sarina's gaze for the length of a curt, kind nod. Ben traces the lip of his wineglass. "Where did that come from, the whole keeping-up-with-the-Joneses thing?"

"The saying?" Bella waves her knife as if this were an obvious question. "It's a metaphor for consumerism."

"But why is it so hard to keep up with them, specifically?"

"Because they keep buying new shit!" Bella says.

"But who are the Joneses?" he persists.

Michael wags an asparagus spear at Ben. "Everyone in my office."

"Everyone is the Joneses," Bella says. "Michael's office, ex-boyfriends, even we are the Joneses."

"So," Georgie concludes, "we are all trying to keep up with ourselves!"

Claudia compliments Georgie on the meal. The table lifts off to another topic, but Ben feels they've left the Joneses prematurely. Sarina watches him mull over ways to return to it. She innately knows his moods and tendencies, the way you know on a flight, even with your eyes closed, that a plane is banking.

Bella is a girl who doesn't mean to be rude ever but is rude, always, and when she asks Sarina if she is still teaching fifth grade, she places on the word *still* a sour sound Claudia hastens to refurbish by saying, "Teaching is so . . ." Only Claudia is a girl who can never procure the right word in a timely manner and during each second she tries, everyone at the table treads water until Ben places his fork down and declares, ". . . noble."

Sarina gazes at him as if he has just returned from war.

Georgie and Michael call out other things teaching is: underpaid, thankless, long-houred, which Michael insists is a word. Emboldened by the support, Sarina embarks on the First Story of the Night.

"It can be emotionally demanding," she begins. "For example . . ." All heads swivel toward her. For the first time, she can see everyone's face at once. The footing of her thoughts slips.

Tell it with confidence, she thinks. Today they made caramel apples in class! Build expectation:

133

How she visited several sweet shops to test caramel. How she double-checked that there was a meaty apple for every child, bought specially sized paper bags to wrap each one after it hardened. How her children took up their reading hour asking questions about the apples. *Do their voices,* she thinks. Sarina gathers the characters in her mind. Madeleine: the nine-year-old who recently lost her mother. Denny: the entitled kid from a well-known family in the parish. She will point out contradictory traits in each kid to offset expectations and her own biases. How Madeleine can be blunt to the point of hurting other children. How Sarina spent an hour holding bawling Denny when the goldfish died. Some characters will play important roles. Some will seem unimportant until the end. If she tells it correctly, when she reaches the Crucial Moment, everyone at the table will feel sickened and satisfied. Sure, she's back in her hometown teaching grade school and she can't fill out the tops of most dresses, but she can tell stories, goddammit. Certainly that must mean something to Ben, she means, men, she means, the universe. Certainly she can cash in a little girl's pain for respect at a dinner party. She will rise from the table, an eagle beating back a glorious pair of wings.

"Just today," she begins, "one of my children got sent home with lice—"

"Lice!" Bella interrupts. "Uck!"

"Lots of children get lice," Claudia says.

"Name one child you know that has lice."

"Me," says Claudia. "Me as a child had lice."

Sarina attempts to regain control. "I can speak from someone who had personal experience as recently as today that lice is—"

Ben laughs. "Me had lice."

Claudia thinks Ben is taunting her for the lice, not the grammar of her sentence. "It means I had thick hair," she says.

Sarina, slipping, falling. "Madeleine has thick hair. The girl who had to be sent home today—"

The table splinters into two preoccupations. Bella asks if her school is the one on Christian with the mural of that sociopath Frank Rizzo. Ben and Michael rejoin the Joneses conversation.

Sarina speaks loudly to get everyone back. "It is a very sad story."

"Would anyone mind if I ate the last of the potatoes?" Georgie says.

"Go right ahead, Georgie. They're your potatoes in the first place."

"They're everyone's potatoes," says Michael.

"As long as no one thinks they're small potatoes," Georgie says.

The table laughs vigorously at what Sarina thinks is a dumb joke. A window closes. As if the party had only one available slot for a long story and her chance has been lost in chatter about shampoo and potatoes. She is striped with a familiar self-loathing around Georgie, left over from high school. Even though she has lived on three continents, Sarina has not progressed further than senior prom. Boys cross rooms for Georgie, who is full in the way they like. *Foxy* is the word for it, Sarina thinks, whereas she is foxless.

Sarina has a flicker of hope when Bella turns to her, taking in a deep breath signifying an important thought. "Isn't teaching grade school not far off from babysitting?"

Sarina forks the last of her salad. "These greens are transcendent."

"Arugula!" Georgie says.

"Let's admit," Ben says. "We keep up with the Joneses to distract us from the fact that we are all going to die!"

"Hear, hear," says Michael.

Dinner is over.

Bella pushes herself away from the table. She has spent the meal wanting more of everything and not taking more of anything. She and Georgie carry empty plates to the kitchen.

Michael says, "I can't keep my hands away from the piano any longer."

Ben says, "Would anyone mind if I stepped outside to call Annie?"

Claudia receives directions to the bathroom.

The room reshuffles and when it stills, Sarina is alone. She hears Michael in the next room fumbling in the pockets of the piano bench, setting up sheet music, and then the first few measures of a splashy intro.

When she saw Ben unwinding his scarf at the front door, Sarina wanted to remove her glasses. She removes her glasses when anything wonderful or embarrassing happens, like earlier today when her principal forced her to discipline Madeleine. Which would have been the Crucial Moment of her story.

Sarina has rebuilt her life one element at a time. The apartment, the job, the easel. It might be a plain life (she occasionally worries she is hiding out in it), but at least it is forged out of what she wants.

She doesn't know the particulars of Ben's wife's job, but it involves legally representing poor kids with leukemia. Show-off. She'd hoped he wouldn't marry the cardiganed girl he brought around four years ago. She'd hoped the girl would be one of the many partners his group rotated in and out. Certainly he would notice how Annie rolled her eyes at his ideas, especially the last idea, when he decided to quit law and pursue screenwriting. Certainly the girl with a flounder's sense of style wouldn't be the one he'd marry on an archipelago in the Caribbean, so Sarina had heard, accessible only by duck boat. But, he did. And, she wasn't. And, he didn't. So, she was.

Outside, the stars have been caught in the act.

Ben paces the stoop ". . . later than I thought. More fun than I expected. No one thought it was strange. Well, yes, they asked how you were but they didn't follow up."

In the kitchen, Georgie and Bella pass a joint back and forth. Bella trains her eyes on the swinging door. "Claudia doesn't know I still smoke. I'm sorry she's acting like a bitch tonight."

At the piano, Michael thinks, there should be words to classical songs.

In the bathroom, Claudia reads a newspaper article about a famous chef's third restaurant opening.

Under the stars, Ben says, "I realize it doesn't count as a separation if we talk on the phone, but you asked me to call you."

In the kitchen, Bella says, "She cut out drama from her life. Now she gets dramatic about people being dramatic."

Georgie says, "It's like ex-smokers who hate smokers."

"Exactly!" Bella says. "Have a cigarette and get over yourself." She shakes her head and pretends to have a new thought. "Sarina has gotten so thin. Poor girl." She wants Georgie to agree, but Georgie has outgrown camaraderie through cattiness.

At the piano, Michael sings, *The more I see you* . . .

Upstairs, Claudia washes her hands with the no-shenanigans soap of a second bathroom. Her interest in the evening's goings-on ranks as follows:

1. How much did Michael's new car cost? She wants to know so she can go home and hate him.
2. She is proud her girlfriend has the ability to introduce lively topics of conversation. Who are the Joneses, indeed?
3. If Alfred Hitchcock were to direct this dinner party, he would have the camera soar in through the window over the gardened patio, through the wings of the expressive drapes, panning to each guest in a way that would convey to the audience that something is terribly wrong.
4. Food is boring. People who use it to feel better than others are worthless. Like Ben's half-hour explanation about the wine. Did he shit the bottle of wine out? That would garner an explanation.

KITCHEN: Georgie says, "I never thought I would get divorced. Never. Divorce is for sad people."

PIANO: Michael sings, *the more I want you . . .*

FAMILY ROOM: Sarina sits, orphaned by the dinner party. What she holds most against these people is how obvious it is that they love each other. A substantive love that caulks the cracks of their personalities; Georgie's oblivion, Bella's self-obsession, Michael's namby-pamby-ness. Sarina hates the part of herself that wants inside that love. A gray, whiskered face appears by her elbow. She replaces her glasses. "Hello, Pepper."

STARS: Ben wipes his eyes with the hand that is not holding the phone. The conversation has ended. Across the street a dog sniffs a signpost. Connected to him via leash is a little boy. Connected to the little boy via hand is The Dad. Ben wants to call to them and wave. He wants the man to nudge his son to wave back. Then Ben could yell *hello* over the empty street. *"What's your dog's name?"* *"Jeb,"* the man would yell. *"Jeb?"* Ben would say, laughing. The man would point to his son. *His idea.* That man could be him, Ben thinks, that little boy could be his, the dog, too. He could be the one yelling *"Jeb!"* across the street to the man wincing through a phone call with his estranged wife. If she had ever liked dogs. Or kids.

Michael stumbles on a wrong note. He tries again. Still wrong. Wrong. Wrong.

In the first week of their marriage, Ben and Annie made three decisions: to install a home security system, to never have children, and to never, ever take salsa lessons. All three were meant to preserve what they owned.

The salsa lessons were Ben's hard line. There was a dance studio on his walk home from the law office. At night it was filled with desperate, churning couples, wagging themselves across the floor.

Whose idea was the kids? Ben wonders, turning to walk inside. He recalls the subject of children being lobbed into the air, Annie saying her flat stomach was her greatest achievement, then taking a call in the other room. The following day the security service arrived to measure the walls.

Ben halts at the window. Inside, Sarina scratches the ears of an earnest-looking cat. Pretty hands, Ben thinks, pretty lap. His breath makes clouds. How long had she been divorced? What had she said about sending a child home for having lice? How was lice the child's fault?

Michael has found the right note and, la-la-la-ing, rejoins the melody.

Claudia returns to the family room and drapes herself over a chair. "I'm sorry Bella is being such a bitch tonight."

"I hadn't noticed," Sarina says.

"You're sweet."

Georgie and Bella return holding plates and forks, with Ben following, clapping warmth into his arms and legs.

My arms won't free you, Michael sings.

"Michael!" Georgie yells. "Quit the piano!" She unveils the key lime pie.

"Extraordinary!" says Sarina.

Michael pats his belly. "Full."

Claudia says, "Couldn't eat one more bite."

Bella gazes at the pie. "Me too. Not another bite."

Georgie frowns. "Sarina?"

"I'll have a piece."

"Me too!" says Ben. "Biggest slice you can."

Sarina and Ben eat the pie. Those who want coffee drink coffee. Occasionally someone sighs. After everyone is finished, Georgie says, "Let's dance."

Bella and Claudia exchange a glance. Michael digs his hands into his pockets and Sarina scrutinizes the carpet.

"It's late," Ben says.

Michael adds, "And we're old."

Georgie thinks about the dishes, the joint she will have after everyone leaves. The quick hush of the extinguished candle.

Bella, Claudia, Michael, and Ben pause on the cold stoop, each considering his or her immediate future. For Bella and Claudia, it is a short walk to their South Street apartment. For Michael, a car ride to the suburbs during which he will have the option of looking at the moon through one of two sunroofs. Ben also has options: he can take a five-minute cab ride to his brownstone in Olde City or he can walk one of the tree-lined streets that connect this part of town to his. It's a good night for a walk. The air is crisp. His wife is staying with her parents indefinitely. His scarf feels good around his neck and his coat is lined in down. Speaking of, where is his scarf?

Inside, Sarina insists she will help with dishes. She wants to avoid good-byes with the others. But Georgie refuses. She reaches over and tucks a strand of hair behind Sarina's ear. "I'm glad you came."

"Me too," Sarina says, coating up. She opens the front door and collides with Ben, who has forgotten his scarf. He disappears inside as she lights a cigarette on the stoop. When he returns, the rest of the party is blocks ahead, too far to run or call out. His forgetfulness and her fear of good-byes have deposited them into this private moment.

Sarina says, "I'm going . . ." and Ben says, ". . . this way," and they point to different directions.

"Please tell Annie I hope she feels better. The flu is going around. Everyone is dropping like flies at school." It is a lie. For once, no illness is circulating the school, though every day she prays something will render Denny absent.

They descend the steps. She thinks his elbow will touch hers but they reach the sidewalk, separate. The brief holiday is over. She says good night and follows the rest of the party.

Behind her, Ben says, "Good night, Sarina."

Good night, Sarina, she thinks. *Because that is my name.* She wants to turn the sound of him saying it into a SEPTA card she can use to get around.

The city is in a perpetual state of being not quite ready to talk about it. Instead it lashes its wind against the banners of the art museum. Moody light changes down Market, the cars bitch toward City Hall. Puddles yearn toward the sewers. The unrequited city dreams up conspiracies and keeps its buildings low to the ground. You are never allowed to dream higher than the hat of William Penn. Dear World, you think you're better than me? Suck a nut. Yours sincerely.

A slip of a woman, trench coated, dips in and out of the shadows on Pine Street, toward the train. Restless wind dissects her.

Good night, Sarina. Good night.

10:00 P.M.

*T*he woman on the phone identifies herself as Diannarah from The Courtland Avenue Club. Her voice is fancy/chintzy.

"I do not wish to disturb you," she says, when Lorca answers. "We have a gentleman here who we ask you to kindly pick up. I want you to understand I am using the term *gentleman* sarcastically as he is feeling up the girls and in general acting like an asshole. We've asked him to leave several times. He says he is an Olympic gymnastics coach, but the license I lifted from his wallet says Max Cubanista. Is he yours?"

"Yes." A new headache blooms at the base of Lorca's skull. "He's mine."

Sonny tells the cold to screw itself. He and Lorca walk to his mustard-colored Buick he thinks can fit into every parking spot in Fishtown. It is crammed between two trucks, its enormous front sticking out into traffic.

Lorca slides into the front seat. "You use a shoehorn?"

Sonny reverses, spins the wheel, accelerates, spins, reverses. Lorca adjusts knobs on the console so heat sighs through the vents. Finally the car is free. Sonny smooths his hair in the rearview mirror and beams.

They ride in silence. Streetlights scan them. What Louisa said about Alex turns in Lorca's mind but doesn't allow him to pinpoint its exact shape or form. "Louisa said Alex is going down a bad road. You know anything about that?"

Sonny's eyes dart from Lorca to the road. He checks his rear view and changes lanes. Light slants in, making him glow. "He's looking skinny," he admits.

"What does that mean?"

The streetlight abandons them, throwing the car into darkness. Sonny sighs. "Come on, Lorc."

"What does that mean? I'm asking."

"I don't know why Louisa has trouble talking to you," Sonny says. "You're such a goddamned peach."

The car clamors over a pothole and part of the ceiling fabric comes undone, making a veil over Lorca's head.

"You got a fix for this?" he says.

Sonny reaches over Lorca and punches the glove compartment open to reveal a staple gun.

"You're a world-class musician," Lorca says. "And your car is held together by string." He shoots staples into the ceiling.

"Do it nice," Sonny says. "Make a line."

146

The Courtland Avenue Club shimmers like a false sunset off the highway. They still have a snake girl. She is featured prominently on a banner that hangs over the entrance. Lorca hasn't been inside in five years. Other than a new coat of paint, not much has changed.

In one of the lanes a group of Main Line girls prepares to bowl, trying out shoes and form-perfect throws. One of them, a rotund, displeased-looking girl, wears a crown with tulle bursting out of it.

"In and out," Lorca says. "Find Max and let's go."

Sonny nods. "You got it."

The door to the strip club is behind the bar. Sonny exchanges words with the bouncer. He tells a joke that only he laughs at, but the bouncer lets him in. Lorca orders a whiskey at the bowling alley's bar. Five years earlier he had stopped in on the way home from scouting a saxophonist in Jersey. Then, it had been Louisa getting his drink and not this girl in the new uniform: a bikini top and shorts.

Lorca swivels to watch the action in the lanes. The place has gained a following among bachelorette parties and hipsters. The yawking group of girls is still testing out grips and throws. One screams, are they ready? The others raise their arms and cheer. They nominate one girl to go to the bar for drinks. She waits for the bartender next to Lorca, so close he can hear her nails tap on the bar. "Are we making complete fools out of ourselves or what?"

"You girls are just right," he says.

She points to the sour-faced girl. "That one is getting married so we drove down from the suburbs."

He raises his glass. "Here's to her."

The girl orders, unfolds several bills from a change purse. Lorca throws a bill to the bartender. The girl attempts to hand it back.

"Please," he says. "Tell your friend I'm happy for her." Even he thinks he sounds desperate.

"I will." She delivers the drinks and comes back. "My friend says thank you."

"Tell her my pleasure."

She takes the stool next to him, mouth knotted in worry. "I've never been to this neighborhood before," she says. Girls were always saying things like this. Like bookmarks, to hold their place until they think of something real to say.

Lorca says, "Where do you live?"

"Princeton. Yardley, actually, but no one's ever heard of Yardley. You ever hear of Yardley?"

"No." He signals the bartender that he wants another, bigger whiskey.

"See?" She fiddles with her scarf and recrosses her legs, revealing the top of one thigh.

The bartender brings his whiskey. He asks the girl what she would like.

This time, she doesn't refuse. "A vodka cranberry."

"Barbara," one of her friends calls. "It's your turn!"

"I'll come back," Barbara says.

There is still no sign of Sonny or Max. Lorca says, "I'll probably be here."

Barbara jogs back to her friends and hurls the ball down the lane. It brings down a few pins. As she waits for her ball to return, one of her friends collects her into a huddle. They giggle, and separate. She throws the ball again with a sound of effort. It brings down the rest of the pins. Her group cheers. In the middle of their hugs she leaps and twirls.

She marks her score and returns to Lorca, hitting a pose. "Was that something or what?"

"That was something."

"My friends are getting jealous." Her breath is sweet with cranberry. "I have to stay with them, or people will say we're in love." She's young, and thinks she has to say pretty things to seem interesting.

"You go with your friends," he says.

"I wish I could stay and talk to you. I sounded ungrateful before. I don't like to feel indebted." At the crux of her collarbone, perspiration grows. She loosens her scarf.

"You were perfect," Lorca says. "Really."

The bartender yells, "Night bowling!" and the

lanes are plunged into black light, revealing iridescent cartoon rabbits high-fiving on the walls. Everything white Barbara wears is glowing. Lorca wears all black. He checks his watch. Val will be into her second set already. They need to get back to the club.

He enters the back room and the door behind him closes, sealing out the noise of the lanes. Topless women wag themselves around a sparkling dance floor. A girl undulates over an elated coed, her expression fuzzed out. In a corner booth, a dancer works on Sonny, his hands clamped on her ass. A pop song belches out of the speakers. Lorca doesn't see Max.

"Where is he?" Lorca mouths.

Sonny points to a farther booth and signals that everything is okay.

Hurry up, Lorca mouths, and leaves. In the bathroom behind the lanes, he pats water onto his forehead. In the hall he collides with Barbara. "Goody," she says. She clasps his wrist and leads him into the ladies' room, where everything is the color of salmon.

She presses her mouth into his neck, feeling for his arms and hair.

"This is much nicer than the men's room," he says. She slides her hands underneath the waistband of his jeans. "Whoa," he says, as if he is bringing a horse to a halt.

She tilts her head. "You don't want to?"

150

"Do I want to?" he says.

He tries to undo her shirt, but the buttons are too small. She does it for him. She hitches up her skirt and spins so he can see her ass. He unclasps her bra. The bathroom's lamp casts dirty blond light onto her bare skin. She wrenches his belt off, his pants down. She holds the top of the stall with delicate hands and he pushes into her.

A nagging sound from the fluorescent bulbs and the hard thrum of the club's music.

"How are you soft everywhere?" he says.

"I know a guy." She wants him to move into her hard. Her lips fill with blood. "Wait," she says.

They are pressed against the stall but sliding toward the ground. Something inside him waits, but something else continues. It gathers and advances.

"Good things come to those who wait," she says, in the pretty way that suddenly seems cruel. His shoulders tremble with effort. Then the quaking recedes and becomes one limitless thing. His thoughts jump off a cliff.

She says, "Go."

It's too late. He is slack.

"No," she says. "Really?"

He tries to force his body to cooperate. He reminds himself of her neck, her nipples. It's no use. They stay together for another moment, making a wishbone on the hard floor. Then she breaks away and he slumps in the corner near the toilet.

"It's no biggie," she says, before he has time to apologize. She pulls up her underwear and skirt and reapplies lipstick in the mirror.

"Where do you live again?" he says.

"A town near Princeton."

"Lucky town near Princeton."

"Yeah." Her voice is filed down, bored. Shame heats him. Someone pounds on the door. Lorca and the girl fix themselves.

Sonny stands in the catastrophe of the hallway. "We need to get Max out of here now."

10:05 P.M.

Madeleine is dreaming. Her apartment is a funeral parlor/nightclub/coffee shop, and also the waiting room at her doctor's office. Her mother lies in a casket filled with apples. Onstage, Billie Holiday sings into a microphone. Her head is a caramel apple.

After announcing her intention to do so, Madeleine walks from the dream kitchen to the dream bedroom to find a roach the size of a fist smoking one of her menthols at a café table on her bureau.

She runs for a can of bug spray, but the cabinet is empty.

"I've already taken it," the roach says. "Along with your paper towels, napkins, and shoes." A yawn scrabbles his multiple sets of legs. "It appears we are on equal footing."

The hair on Madeleine's arms rises. "Are you the roach I killed today?"

"I'm the roach you thought you killed today. I'm Clarence and I'd like to have a chat." His legs reflect in the mirror behind him, making it seem like there are two of him, one carrying on a conversation with her, and one carrying on a conversation with her reflection. "You are one friendless Susie Q."

Madeleine says she has plenty of friends and Clarence pshaws. "Like who?"

"Like Pedro."

"Pedro!" Puffs of angry smoke. "Who you put on a leash!" A shiver runs through his antennae. "Toots, it's sadsville around here. You've been crying all night with that thing on your nose. What is there to be so miserable about?"

Madeleine's hand covers her clothespin. "I got yelled at by everyone today," she says. "I want to sing and no one will let me."

A sound like a clarinet reverberates from what she assumes to be his head, a jeering, mocking sound. "Where do you think I would be if I listened to every 'Get out of here' or 'Call the Realtor, we're moving.' You're just a human being. Pathetic, stiff. Not one of you is worth even the tiniest grain of rice. It's time to grow a set of balls. Learn how to say, 'fuck it.' Otherwise, you're never going to leave the house, like Old Mr. So and So . . ." He hitches a foot toward her father's room. "You don't want that, do you?"

Madeleine says no.

He glowers. "It used to be fun here. Music all the time and singing."

"My mother died."

Clarence sighs. "Just because your mother is dead doesn't give you the right to suck."

"How do you know Pedro?" she says.

He shrugs several shoulders. Madeleine shrugs, too.

"Everyone knows Pedro." He extinguishes his cigarette on the top of Madeleine's bureau and, with a sound like a paper tearing, dives into a crack in the wall.

10:06 P.M.

*C*ertainly, however (an older couple asks, is this Spruce Street?), Sarina thinks, he didn't have to (Sarina says yes) say my name. He could have called out an unaddressed (Spruce Street, they ask, not Spruce Road?) salutation in the night. Every night (Sarina says yes, there is no such thing as Spruce Road) hundreds of people call out good night to no one. (Thank you, the couple says, have a good night!) Good morning! Good afternoon! The word *Sarina* was a choice. Good night, Sarina. Good night.

Sarina walks to the station. She will process the party only when she has secured a seat on the train. In the relief of her home, she will throw her keys into a bowl, gather her hair into an elastic, and eat ice cream and cherries while watching the news. His lucky scarf. How his neck bears a freckle the shape of Florida that specifies his neck as his. The years had clarified his handsomeness, hadn't they? When he said good night he sounded regretful, didn't he?

Outside the store, bucketed roses grin under heat lamps. The man behind the counter tosses her the cigarettes without looking up from his newspaper.

Two teenagers shuffle up and down the aisles.

"It's my mom's boyfriend," one of them says, "and I work for him. But I said, 'You tell me what to do on-site, you can't tell me what to do at home.'"

"Matches?" says the man behind the counter.

"Please," Sarina says.

"It's cold out," he says. "Do you enjoy the winter?"

"I prefer the hot." She organizes the coins in her coin purse, the bills in the billfold.

"I did too when I was young." He goes back to his paper.

"I wish I'd hit him with that pipe," says the teenager whose mother dates his boss. "But then I'd be in jail, I guess." They sidle up behind her and their talk ceases. This means they are sizing up her ass. She turns to catch them, but they are engrossed in a comic book. No one is admiring her ass.

Outside, Sarina considers buying a sleeve of roses. She evaluates each bunch then walks to the station.

There is time before the next train, so she has a cigarette on the platform. She can see the brick homes of Olde City. The dumb scratch of moon. When the train heaves and pumps into the station, Sarina realizes she has forgotten her wallet at the store with the roses and teenagers. She runs. Her low heels thwack against the pavement.

Ben, frowning over a pack of Camel Reds, looks at the girl who has entered, a beautiful girl who is flushed from running, she is familiar, it is Sarina: he is still frowning, so Sarina pauses in the doorway thinking he is upset with her until a smile he could not have planned opens on his face.

He raises his hands in mock penance. "I needed a cigarette."

"I forgot my wallet," she says.

Ben pays. Sarina wants the store owner to wink or refer to their previous exchange so Ben thinks she has charming conversations throughout the night with whomever, whenever. The store owner does not participate.

Outside, the teenagers read the comic book under a streetlight.

Sarina nods toward them. "Those guys are trouble."

Ben considers them. He lights her cigarette before his own. "I'll walk you to the train."

Sarina wants to walk with Ben to the train more than she wants peaceful old age. "No, thank you," she says. "It's only a few blocks."

"I can either stand here and have this cigarette or walk. It's all the same."

"Then walk me," she says.

They walk.

"Parrots live in this neighborhood," he says. "I saw one a few weeks ago. Honest-to-God parrots."

"I don't believe you."

"Annie didn't believe me either. But still, they're there. Someone must be feeding them."

"Right there?" She points to a tree. As if on command, no parrots appear. Ben takes a drag of his cigarette.

Sarina takes a drag of hers. "Michael's singing is getting better."

"Yes, let's talk about Michael's singing."

Is he drunk or just being silly? Sarina plays along. "He reaches notes only dogs can hear."

"He came over last week and sang at my house," he says. "When he left, my clocks were two hours slow."

"His tone sends helicopters off course."

"But his delivery is perfect."

"Flawless," Sarina says. A limo slinks by, the shouts of a bridal party. "I have a special fondness for Michael. He was my only dance at senior prom, you realize."

Ben winces. "I know."

They reach the station and extinguish the hope of their cigarettes. Ben collects both and deposits them into a nearby trash can. That was a careless thing to do, she thinks, bringing up the prom. If he wants to talk more, she will talk. Even though that means she will miss the 10:30 and have to wait for the 11:00.

Saying good-bye to Ben is Sarina's least favorite activity. So sad the number of times she's had to do it. Ball games, recitals, the homes of friends, rented shore houses, through car windows after dropping off some forgotten camera to Annie. *Good-bye. See you later. Nice seeing you.* She has mastered it: A dismissive peck on the cheek. A hug like an afterthought. Telling herself, *Do not watch him walk away*. Watching him walk away. Watching him drive away. Watching him descend the stairs to the subway. How many times have they said good-bye to each other? Already tonight, twice.

He interrupts her before she can get the second good-bye out.

"How would you feel," he says, "about missing your train?"

Once at the beach, Sarina watched a crane bathing in a gully at dusk. It used its wings to funnel the water over its back, then shook out the excess in a firework of droplets. After several minutes it took off, arcing out over the fretless sea. That felt like this.

10:10 P.M.

Max Cubanista is a liar's liar and no matter what he tells you he did not invent the radio. He is not "Chuck Berry's only living pupil." He's never waylaid an armed robbery by playing music for the thieves. He was not the inspiration for the song "They Can't Take That Away from Me." He does not own a bungalow in Havana. He and the Cubanistas are as Cuban as a pack of hot dogs. On most nights Max sleeps on the floor of Lorca's back room next to a pile of his own sick.

Now he dozes in a booth at The Courtland Avenue Club. Every so often his chin finds a resting place on his chest, bringing him back to life, hurling insults at the girls standing over him and at Sonny and Lorca, who attempt to rouse him.

One of the dancers covers her naked breasts with her hands. "Tell your friend he's an asshole."

"He's right here." Lorca hitches his arm under Max's armpit. "Tell him yourself."

The girl leans into Max. "You're an asshole."

Max's eyes are closed. "You're a dear to say so."

Lorca and Sonny hang Max between them and make slow progress through the room. The topless girl follows them, still yelling, stopping when they reach the door to the lanes, as if cordoned off by an unseen fence. Her friend tosses her a shirt. *Cape May,* it reads, *the most haunted town in America!*

They carry Max past Barbara, who waves the fingers of one hand as they go by, and through the doors to the parking lot. When they reach the car, Lorca realizes they are being followed by a girl in yellow heels.

"I'm Daphne." She points to Max. "He promised me a ride."

"A ride to where?" Sonny says.

"The Cat's Pajamas."

"What a coincidence," Lorca positions Max unkindly in the backseat. "That's exactly where we're going."

During the ride, Max outlines his thoughts: He wants a sandwich, he is getting the Christ scratched out of him by the seat belt, he doesn't see what the big deal is.

Lorca smells Barbara on his hands. Desk chair and heavy cream. He went limp on her, so he will go back to his club and get drunk before Mongoose arrives. A flute begins in his gut. Every light on the street turns green.

The tables are filled when they return and Valentine is halfway through her second set. She lifts her eyes from the violin strings to watch them haul Max through the club. They deposit him onto a cot in the back room and Sonny gallops down the hall to join Valentine onstage.

Lorca removes a flask from his top drawer. Max pulls a joint out from an unseen place under the cot.

"You go on in twenty minutes," Lorca reminds him.

Max exhales. "I might be a little late."

"We close at two tonight. Not one second later. If I have to turn off the electricity and pull you from that stage, I will."

Max leaps from the cot and growls into a hanging mirror. "You're scared, brother. But we'll figure out a way to pay that citation."

"Sonny told you?"

"I guessed." He slaps his face and yowls. "Is anybody ready to rock and roll?"

Lorca leaves Max yowling in the back room to catch Val's last song. She is an old-timer violinist and had been one of his father's closest friends. Her hair is arranged in its familiar braid. Her considerable hands and arms make the violin appear dainty. She plays Stéphane Grappelli while Sonny chugs underneath her. "I'll Never Be the Same." There are enough people in the club so that not everyone has a seat but not enough that you can't see the stage. This is Lorca's favorite part of the night.

Valentine's pianist rolls octaves at the top of the piano. Her gaze lifts to meet Sonny's, but he's not a smiler. Here and there he gives her a civilized tremolo. There is no better technical guitarist than Sonny. Tight, chaste solos. Reasonable quotations. City musicians regularly call on him for studio sessions because he is reliable and even. If he promises something at the beginning of a riff, he delivers. However with age his hold on the pitch has slackened. It started with a note or phrase, occasional enough to seem like a fluke. Now it happens regularly. Lorca can jibe Sonny for his retreating hairline, his bullshit parking, his emphatic, misguided directions, but never this: that when his old friend plays he holds his breath, anticipating an errant sound, the way he does when newbies try the stage.

Cassidy swings a bottle of rum to meet a glass.

"Swing one around for me," Lorca says.

Alex sulks on one of the stools with Aruna Sha, in another mutinous dress. The ash on her cigarette grows and menaces over the clean floor. Their occasional Main Line hanger-on is with them, a friend whose name Lorca always forgets. The kid yearns to be Alex, this is clear in the way he orbits him, undercutting anything he says. He jaws on about jazz, the one time he saw a famous musician.

"You can't smoke in here, honey," Lorca says.

Aruna drops her cigarette into Alex's beer. She searches her bag, then she and the Main Line kid disappear into the back. After a moment, Alex follows.

Val swings her bow up for the final, shivering G.

She holds it for several seconds as Sonny picks out the final chords. The audience applauds and makes demands but Val ignores them, so many of them go outside to smoke in the lull between acts.

The Cubanistas set up: Max on vocals and lead guitar, Gus on timbales, Sonny on keyboards, and Emo Sonofabitch Gladden on trumpet. Two of Emo's friends sit in on percussion, congas and cajón. The Cubanistas have a following, mostly professors from the university having affairs, university kids studying South American culture, or women bowled over by the pidgin Spanish of a Cubanista brother.

Max has donned the Cubanista uniform: beige riding pants slashed indiscriminately with pink sequins, faded button-down, beige band jacket. He skips sound check to snow the girl in yellow heels. Owner of the Club is his favorite put-on. It seems to require sweating and pelvic thrusts. Perspiration pumps down his cheeks from his orderly Afro. As long as he brings in a crowd, Lorca doesn't care who he lies to.

"I do sets on Friday nights, they'd have me play *eeev-ery* night if I could, Lorca's a madman, but I tell *heem,* sometimes I have to do paperwork and filing, there's a lot that goes into *ronning* a club."

"Of course you can't play every night when you run a club," she says, elongating the last word into a concerned three syllables. "What's a Lorca?"

"That's a Lorca." Max gestures to Lorca as if he is leftovers. "My right-hand man. He's *bean* with me since the beginning. Together we turned this pile of cheese into the best jazz club in the world."

She swivels to Lorca as if he is a mirror to check her hair. "I thought the best jazz club in the world was Mongoose's."

Max pouts. "Dar-leeng, no. Mongoose's is a trash castle. You hear about the band he has playing for him now? What are they called? The traveling . . . something . . . The Triangles."

"The Troubadours," Lorca says. "It's the same house band with a different name. Rico and the boys."

"Naw," Max stretches his leg on a stool. "It's something like the Triangles." The girl's attention drifts to the stage, where Gus is warming up. "In any case, darling, they're frauds." He nuzzles the girl's neck. She waves him off. He continues the tour, pointing to where the Snakehead hangs. "That's the Snakehead I won in a card game with Steve Earle."

"What's a Snakehead?" the girl says.

"It's like a classic Mustang, doll, only rarer and older."

She is unimpressed. "It does seem faded and creaky, like old things do."

Lorca, Sonny, and Max straighten on their stools. "Are you going to warm up?" Sonny says. "Or are you going to stand here playing tour guide?"

Someone has barred the men's bathroom door shut. A line forms in the hallway.

"It's been, like, fifteen minutes," one of the men notifies Lorca.

Lorca knocks. A commotion inside, a dropped plastic thing, and a curse. Lorca pounds. The door unlatches and Alex, Aruna, and the friend appear. Alex pushes past his father into the hallway. The men who have been waiting shuffle inside. Alex leans over the bar and smiles for a drink. He taps out a beat on his thighs. Gus catches a cymbal in midgasp. Aruna reaches for his hand. Lorca sees that his son is skinny, not in a lean way but in the way Sonny alluded to in the car. He cannot remember the last time he had a meal with his son. He cannot remember the last time he saw Alex eat anything. The sun-colored fingertips, the mottled bruises on his son's forearms. Alex's shape comes into searing focus, as if Lorca's eyes have taken sixteen years to adjust to new light.

10:50 P.M.

Near the fountain at Rittenhouse Square Park, Sarina evaluates a display of pinwheels whirling in planets of green foam. "How much for the red?" she asks the man selling them.

"Five," he says.

"Yikes. And the yellow?"

"Six."

She narrows her eyes. "Why is the yellow more than the red?"

"Bigger," he says.

Ben takes a seat on the edge of the fountain. Sarina will deliberate until she ultimately opts against buying a pinwheel. He innately knows her moods and tendencies the way you know on a flight, even with your eyes closed, that a plane is banking.

Sarina blows into the yellow pinwheel. The man says, "Every year they perform *A Christmas Carol* here in the square. Have you ever seen it?"

"Scrooge?"

"It's about rich people being assholes. Every year, here, where the richest people in the city live."

"Irony," Sarina says.

"Do you think any of them realize what they're watching?"

"I thought the richest people lived on the Main Line." Sarina replaces the pinwheel. "I guess they can afford a five-dollar pinwheel."

He sniffs. "My prices are market."

Ben hurls one leg over the side of the fountain, then the other. The cold realization of the water pauses him. He tromps toward the other side.

"What's he doing?" the pinwheel man says.

Sarina doesn't answer but doffs her heels and leaps the wall. Knee-deep. She pushes through the cold water to catch up.

On the other side of the fountain, a woman wearing a sequined hat calls out, "Hello! I know you!" She waves to Ben, who lifts his hand in a half salutation.

"You do?" he says.

"I know you! You were my husband's lawyer. Bill Evans. That's my husband's name. You helped him when he got hurt at work. A beam fell on his head. You got us a nice settlement. Oh, bless you. I do know you. I do."

Ben is calf-deep in water. "How is Bill these days?"

"He's good, yes."

"Working?"

"Oh no," she says.

"No," Ben says.

"It's tough."

"I know."

"Of course you do. Bless you." She nods at

169

Sarina. If she is surprised to see two adults wading through fountain water on a bitter night she doesn't show it. "Bless you both."

"Tell Bill hello," Ben says.

"I will." The woman wrenches something out of her bag, a wrapper or a slip of paper, beelines for a trash can where she reconsiders. She calls out, "He'll be thrilled!"

They watch her leave the square.

"Bill Evans," Ben says. He pretends to notice his pant legs. "Good heavens, I'm drenched!"

Sarina giggles.

Ben hurdles the wall of the fountain. He takes Sarina's hand and helps her climb out. For a moment they are two people holding hands. He lets go.

"We can't stand here cold and wet," he says. "We should go somewhere and dry off."

"And get a drink," she adds, slipping into her shoes.

"I know just the place."

"Good-bye!" Sarina calls to the pinwheel man.

"Good luck," he says.

"Tell me about the girl with lice," Ben says, as they walk out of the park onto Pine Street.

Pine Street maintains a long-standing race: how many apartments, houses, and stores can one street hold? There are no zoning restrictions: go! When each stoop or store window has a lamp on, the effect is akin to the after-hours daylight of a nuclear power plant. Sarina and Ben walk through this unnatural sunshine as she details the singing, the principal, Clare Kelly, the apples, the lice, the punch, the expulsion. She does not look at him while she talks. She already knows what she will see, so what's the point? An open, happy mouth. Hazy, engaged eyes. Big deal.

Ben does not look at Sarina. He already knows what he will see. The line around her mouth that appears when she is intent on exposing injustice: the cockamamie price of pinwheels or unfairness toward one of her students. A girl in constant negotiation with her bangs. She giggled when he said, "Someone has drenched my pant leg!" Her laugh has always been the only ungoverned thing about her. He tries to elicit it as much as he can.

A bookstore on the corner is open. They hear tinkling music inside.

"Should we go in?" Ben says.

"Let's."

Inside, whatever is not wreathed is tinseled. A knitting older woman behind the counter regards them through reading glasses. "It's right there," she says, pointing to a display table stacked with books. On the cover, a dragon gives a thumbs-up. *Sunshine the Dragon Joins the Circus!* "You're here for the launch, right?"

"We couldn't wait," Ben says.

"You and everybody else." The woman motions

behind them. Sarina and Ben turn around. No one is in the doorway.

"Would it bother you if we browsed?" Ben says.

"Very little bothers me." The woman returns to her knitting.

The bookstore has three large rooms separated by archways. Sarina waits until Ben has chosen a book to sneak a glance at him; he does not like the edition and returns it, stalks through the archway to the other room and picks up another book, then, faking an errand to his right, sneaks a glance at Sarina.

"We're closing soon," the woman says.

"Give us a preview," Ben says. "What's the dragon do in this one?"

"No previews," she says. The needles make plastic thwacking sounds.

"Scarf?" Ben guesses.

"Sweater," she says. "For my cat."

"Lucky cat," Ben says.

"He runs away with the circus."

"Your cat?" says Sarina.

"Sunshine the Dragon."

"He does not," Ben says.

"What would be my motivation to shit you? He sells popcorn and funnel cake. His dream is to become a trapeze artist but he's a dragon so he's too heavy. His weight would snap the trapeze."

"Can't he fly?" Ben says.

The woman approves. "Now you're using your noggin."

Ben produces his wallet. "Ring us up for one, please."

They return to the street.

"Do you think Sunshine the Dragon will learn trapeze?" Sarina says.

"I have a feeling everything is going to be fine." Ben winks.

Sarina's blush swells from her neck into her cheeks. They reach the place he knows, a cigar bar in the basement of a restaurant. She no longer cares about the train. She will take a cab. Or sleep in a stairwell on a pile of rats.

"What is going to happen to that little girl?" Ben says.

Sarina knows he means Madeleine, who she hopes is home, sleeping under a heavy blanket. She speaks with an optimism she doesn't feel. "Everything is going to be fine."

11:00 P.M.

Mark Altimari stands in the doorway of Madeleine's bedroom, watching her sleep. Her fists are clenched beneath her chin as if even in dreams she must protect herself against foes.

Corrine, Madeleine's mother, is in the kitchen, making one of their simple dinners. Mark can hear her distracted singing. Madeleine is three.

Mark wants to drink wine and dance to his new record. He wants to palm his wife's full rump. He wants to order pizza. But Corrine believes in saving money, in slow meals and something to eat while you're cooking them. She cuts slices out of a peach while the sauce simmers. Billie Holiday plays. Mark flips through his record collection to select the next album.

They are good at being together. Leaving space. Leaving notes. Bringing home slabs of Locatelli, her favorite cheese. His tangy smell.

They were in the first wave of young couples to settle near Ninth Street, bringing new energy to the Old World market. Mark would have preferred a house in the country but Corrine said the city would be their daughter's best teacher. They bought a shop and Mark sold handmade cheeses. Corrine manned the cash register and worked at The Courtland Avenue Club at night. They were respectful of the other shop owners, who in some cases had been there for fifty years. Their business grew so Mark bought another shop, across town. Then another. Walking home every night, a wedge of Locatelli or a fistful of lavender tucked into his apron pocket, he tried to shake the dread fortune produced.

Corrine's knife stills, as if she has detected a kink in the air. "What's that sound?" she says.

Mark places his nose in the space where her shoulder meets her neck. Steals a slice from the cutting board. "No sound, dear."

"Listen," she insists.

Billie Holiday's voice has been twinned. He looks to the record player for explanation.

"You don't think," she says, but interrupts herself to place her finger over her lips. He lowers the volume. Billie's voice recedes. The other gets louder. It is coming from Madeleine's bedroom, but it couldn't be their daughter, who has yet to say her first word. She doesn't seem interested in talking and trails kids her age in verbal skills.

I hear music, mighty fine music . . .

A gust of air, a sudden shove. As if all of the house's atoms had been paused on the brink of propulsion and this is their cue. The silverware drawer bursts out of its track. The forks and spoons rise into the air. The plate lifts, each peach slice orbiting it like a private solar system.

Corrine releases her grip on the knife. It stays in the air. She turns her shocked eyes to Mark.

The singing is unworried and clear. The saucepan lurches, in fits and starts leaving its heated place, skirts the stovetop, and falls to the ground. Corrine lunges to catch it but misses. The sauce ruins itself over her arms. She squeaks and plunges them under the faucet's cold water.

The glasses in the cupboards, the cookbooks, the recipe box, hover a foot off their perches. The dish towels ascend above their wooden rods.

"What is this?" Corrine says.

The voice is oblivious to the mayhem it's causing.

Mark stumbles into the back bedroom to find their baby clutching the bars of her crib. She is singing. He halts, scared to approach this unfamiliar creature. Madeleine holds the last, joyful note. Mark lifts her out of her crib and returns to the family room, where everything is collapsing. Corrine dodges the kitchen items that have been abandoned by their arrangements with gravity. Mark silences the music.

Finally, everything is still. They gape at Madeleine, who bounces and claps in Mark's arms. "Order a pizza?" Mark says finally.

Corrine laughs. "What I wanted to begin with."

When Madeleine sings, everyone gets what they want.

Almost everyone.

Every morning Mark wakes up thinking Corrine is still alive. Every morning he finds her side of the bed empty and suffers the loss again.

Madeleine has her mother's formidable nose, the brown eyes that always seem on the verge of tears. Mark wants to love his daughter, but being around her makes him miss his wife more. Madeleine is only what is left. Mark glides a book underneath his sleeping daughter's hand. *History of Jazz, Volume Two*. When she wakes, at least there will be something good waiting.

11:05 P.M.

Lorca palms his son's shoulder. "Come outside with me and smoke a cigarette."

Alex blanches at his father's touch. Laughter shivers through his friends. "I'm fine, Pop."

"Alex," Lorca says.

Aruna says she'll come too, but Lorca stops her. "You will stay here in this bar while I go outside to speak with my son." He leads Alex through the vestibule where well-dressed people fight their coats off. He rattles his pack, but Alex doesn't want one. The Second Street Bridge is lit in green and red. Alex is taller than him but would be no match for a gust of wind.

Lorca remembers what it's like to be sixteen and feel bigger than the city. "You coming by on Christmas?"

Alex doesn't meet his father's eyes. "Of course, Pop."

He has practiced this aloofness, but Lorca knows he cries at movies if an animal is injured. "I'll cook. Roast chicken."

"Since when do you cook?" Alex says.

"Since never."

"Will Louisa be there?"

Lorca kicks at the grass snarling out of the sidewalk. "Louisa left me."

178

"She told me," Alex says.

In the doorway, one girl asks another if there's a cover. "Beats me," her friend says.

"There's no cover," Lorca calls out.

They stop, blondes in tweed coats, and glare at him.

"I know you don't like her," Alex says. "But can I bring Aruna?"

"It's Christmas. Everyone's invited."

"I keep forgetting it's Christmas."

"You and me both." Lorca smells the brine of the river. The swipe of his son's cheap cologne. "A cop came by this morning and told us that unless we pay thousands of dollars the club will be closed."

"Sonny told me," Alex says.

Lorca sighs. "I guess he told everyone."

Alex stiffens at the word *everyone*. "All the same to me," he says. "Not like I can play here anyway."

Lorca has again said the wrong thing, forcing up the wall between them. A pummeled feeling leans against him. In every apartment on every street in this city there are better fathers, but not one of them has a more gifted son. "How old are you?" he says.

"Sixteen."

"How old?"

Alex spits. "Sixteen, Pop. I get it. I'm too young."

"Alex." Lorca's gaze is even. "Someone might

179

ask how old you are tonight and if they do, what do you say?"

Alex swallows hard. "Twenty-four." If he celebrates, his father will change his mind. He innately knows his father's moods and tendencies the way you know on a flight, even with your eyes closed, that a plane is banking. So he races to the door. His hand slips on the handle because his body won't let him go as fast as he wants.

His father calls his name.

Alex turns back to the man smoking on the sidewalk. *Please don't take this away from me.* People jostle by while he hangs in the doorway, waiting for his father to speak.

"Don't get cocky," Lorca says. "I'd go with twenty-one."

Alex vanishes into the club, leaving his father alone on the street.

11:10 P.M.

Ben orders two whiskeys and two Churchills and pats his legs dry with bar napkins. Sarina makes flimsy promises to herself in the ladies' room mirror. She will have one drink, total. Two. She will have two drinks and the third will be water. She will ask about Annie. She will not mention Annie. She will not cross her legs for effect. She will absolutely cross her legs every five seconds. She will not, under any circumstances, call anything "transcendent." She will keep her ever-loving shit together. Even if he touches her cheek. Which he has already done three times. Why does he touch her cheek so much? Is he someone who touches people's cheeks or is it her cheek specifically? She touches her cheek. Not bad.

Here stands Sarina in the mirror of a cigar bar, reminding herself that there is no color skirt she can wear that would make Ben single. There is no way she can fix her hair, no perfume on earth, no story amusing enough. Even if she wishes in this mirror for an hour, this night will end with a good-bye and a bowl of ice cream with cherries. She is obvious and see-through and a joke. She will never leave this bathroom. He'll be confused initially but then will return to his life. She will live here, teach via telephone, knit in the evenings. They will say, *Remember that night Georgie had a dinner party and Sarina decided to live in the bathroom?* She will die here, next to this decorative toilet paper decanter and that vintage cat poster. People will say, they will say, people will say.

A jiggling sound. A stranger tries the door.

Sarina checks her watch.

11:11 P.M.

Madeleine sings into a pale silver microphone, her favorite instrument the stand-up bass running like a low-grade fever in and out of the rooms of her dreams.

In the back room of The Cat's Pajamas, Alex suits up. He wants his father to hear him and know he can play. Not only hear him, but *hear* him.

"No." John McCormick halts his little sister, who was going for the door again.

Jill returns to her chair. She stabs at her wooden duck with a paintbrush filled with Winter Grain Green. It is impossible to concentrate on her mallard when her parents are fighting. Her other brother, Norman, paints the belly of his Northern Pintail with Stone Cottage Gray. John paints his duck with John-like caution. He pauses between applications to consider the ruckus in the other room, or to give a gentle no to his sister, who wants to go in and soothe. But then they'd get in trouble for not being in bed, or worse.

On the other side of the door, their parents use words like *whore* and *dickhead*.

"Do you think my duck is sad?" Jill says.

"North American mallards," John pretends to

read, "are among the world's happiest ducks. When winter comes, they fly in happy families to Latin America."

Jill readjusts her glasses. She considers her duck with this new information. Steve, she's named him. "Steve?" she tests.

The unmistakable sound of a slap makes even John place his brush down on the palette. "Don't go in there," he says, before Jill even leaves her chair.

In the back bedroom of her family's row home, Clare Kelly dozes on her chaise lounge, busted leg propped on a pillow, dreaming of GLORY and THIGH GAPS.

Louisa Vicino heats popcorn on her brother's stovetop. She catches sight of herself in the kitchen window, so serious, shaking kernels in the pan. She gives herself a shimmy. Laughs. Gives herself another shimmy. Unfurls one arm, then the other. She can feel the snakes' smooth, pearlized skins, their buttery breaths on her neck, the pleasant squeeze as they wind around her belly.

Her brother calls from the other room. "How's that popcorn coming?"

Louisa goes into a split on the kitchen's unforgiving floor. Hand flourishes. One last shimmy. Big finish.

• • •

Principal Randles wants a nightcap with the tax attorney. Dinner concludes over two modest pieces of mochi. He slips a credit card into the bill. "Would you like to . . ."

"I would love to," she says.

He is noticeably relieved. "I know just the place."

In the deep moss of cigar smoke, Sarina reglosses her lips and wishes for strength. She switches off the light and closes the door. Ben is where she left him, only now a man in a gray suit is pumping his hand like an oil rig, a man who, Sarina realizes with pain when he pivots to greet her, is her ex-husband, Marcos.

Midnight

Marcos is a man whose cologne precedes him. He runs a successful hedge fund in Connecticut and owns homes on two different beaches in two different countries. Ben had been reading the Sunshine book when Marcos descended upon him. Ben hasn't seen Sarina's overly enthusiastic ex-husband in years and has spent exactly no time weeping over it.

"What luck running into you," Marcos says. "I'm on my way to a truly special place."

Because he knows Marcos can't, Ben says, "Stay for a drink."

Sarina approaches and does not reclaim her stool. Ben has asked her ex-husband to join them which means he does not want to be alone with her. Perhaps he has been hoping for an interruption or planning a demure exit. She hates the moody figure of this night.

"Still doing pro bono work?" Marcos asks Ben. "Pro bono work is so . . ."

". . . noble," Sarina finishes.

Marcos chucks her shoulder. "Still finishing my sentences, hon."

Ben says, "I am still doing pro bono work."

"Too bad." Marcos orders a seven and seven,

hands the bartender a twenty, and tells him to keep the change.

Ben and Sarina sip their drinks.

"Tell me about this special place," Sarina says.

"Truly special," Ben says.

"It's a club with a house band to beat the . . ."

"Band?" Ben offers.

"Oho!" says Marcos.

"Now *I'm* finishing your sentences." Ben downs his drink in a succinct gulp. "We should get married."

Marcos is regularly trailed by the feeling he is being taunted in a way he cannot articulate. He is aware of being intellectually late to every party with pissants like Ben Allen lurking in the periphery, ready to remind him. It doesn't bother Marcos. He has five walk-in closets and a young girlfriend who thinks it's cute to call him Daddy. He enjoys the fact that men like Ben never seem to be able to meet his gaze.

"Where is the club?" Sarina says.

"Fishtown." He cradles the back of an invisible partner. "Dancing."

"Dancing." Sarina looks wistful. "But I wake up early to paint."

"How's it coming?" Marcos says.

"It's coming."

"What are you painting these days?" Ben says. "Still lifes?"

"Not exactly," Marcos says. His and Sarina's

187

shared smile creates a box on the outside of which Ben simpers into his Churchill.

"What's this?" Marcos points to the book.

"A dragon," Sarina says. ". . . Who joins the circus." She holds up a picture of Sunshine selling cotton candy. "See?"

Ben, grateful for the chance to flaunt his knowledge, says, "He also has a friend who is a talking peanut named Sky."

"This is new information!" she says.

"I read it while you were in the bathroom."

Marcos looks from Sarina to Ben. Sarina to Ben. *What is this excitement for children's ephemera, this allusion to shared time?*

Sarina and Marcos had married after a brief, aggressive courtship. He was brawny, cocksure. She was elegant, kooky. He liked the shape they made at parties. As Sarina spent more and more hours in her studio, the brevity of the courting time occurred and reoccurred to Marcos. They were incompatible but he liked her, then and now, very much. Even during the divorce proceedings, she was kind. *What is she doing here with this failed lawyer?* Marcos recalls Ben's pale wife, who had a propensity for poly blends. This is a dangerous situation for Sarina, but Marcos's concern for his ex has a time limit. A nubile redhead waits for him at the other end of the city.

"The Cat's Pajamas," he says. ". . . Is the name

of the club . . . and I must go." He registers Sarina's relief. ". . . Miles to go before I sleep."

"Whitman," Ben says.

Marcos throws a few dollars on the bar. "Frost."

Ben frowns. "I think it's Whitman."

"Well, it's Frost."

"Don't mess with him on American poetry," Sarina says. Marcos beams at her and for a moment, they are still married. Then a redheaded moment takes its place.

"Walk me out," Marcos tells her, shaking hands with Ben. He knows she won't want to, but she will. These are the residual obligations of having been married to someone.

Marcos curses when they reach the street. "I hate this weather." He whistles for a cab. "Let's go to Mexico."

"Can you have me back by Christmas?" Sarina says.

"Skip it," he says. "What are you planning to do for it anyway?"

"My sister's. Her kids. Baked ziti, I guess. Dry chicken."

"The sister." Marcos's tone is playful. "She single yet?"

A cab brakes in front of them. "Good-bye, Marcos," she says.

"What are you doing in there?" He jerks his chin to the bar.

"Having a drink with a friend."

"Is that what you call it?" Marcos gets into the cab and closes the door. The window descends. "Be careful, girl."

Sarina watches the cab leave. She spent most of their two-year marriage in a bathing suit. He could spend an hour kissing her knees. He was his own kind of gentleman. When they were married he would never have been on a two-hour walk with someone else when she was at home sick.

Marcos's knife-through-butter certainty has lifted the evening's scrim. She can no longer act like this is a meaningless walk. She will say good-bye to Ben. It will not be a sorry thing.

As she walks toward him at the bar, Sarina memorizes him. Lanky legs hiked up on the stool as if ready to spring.

His rueful smile stops her. "Annie and I have separated."

Greg Michaelman is getting married in the morning! He and his friends have been staked at a booth in the cigar bar for hours drinking scotch! Greg has already fielded three phone calls from his fiancée, who is upset for reasons he cannot understand! One of his boys decides they need a picture immediately and produces a camera! But who will take it!

Ask her, someone says, and points to the only girl in the bar, a short-haired stick figure sitting with some jag. They are in conversation but there

190

is no conversation more important than taking a picture of Greg Michaelman and his boys!

"Take my picture!" Greg Michaelman yells. "I'm getting married tomorrow."

The girl does not hear, so Greg yells again. She turns, pale with anger. Greg feels the scotch tingle darkly in his throat.

"What is it?" she says.

One of his buddies holds up a camera. "He's getting married tomorrow. Take our picture!"

She accepts the camera. Up close, she is cuter than Greg Michaelman thought.

"You." She points to Rodriguez. "Scootch in. Act like you like each other."

Greg feels the bodies of his friends on either side of him. He has been through school and mud with these boys. There is no town better than his college town, so he never strayed. He has eaten breakfast at all of their kitchen counters. He has watched countless games on countless televisions. He has not always been kind. He didn't show up for Ollie's dad's funeral and he ignored Rodriguez's phone calls after he was laid off. He hasn't exactly comforted Allison when she's griped about her weight. He would like her to lose the handful of flesh that hangs over her underwear's waistband. A flash. The girl takes the picture and Greg Michaelman is certain about one thing: he is going to make Allison Cady happy for the rest of her life.

Sarina hands the camera back to the one with the open shirt, ignores his requests for her number as she walks away. One of them grabs her waist with a rough grip. "Take another one," he commands. "In case that one's not good."

"It's fine," she says. "I checked."

"Don't be a bitch," the groom says.

Sarina takes the camera back. Obediently, they cozy next to each other on the leather couch. "Smile." They oblige. "That's all?" She frowns. "You don't want to get closer? Get closer," she barks. They titter. One of them grabs another's breast, joking. "That's it," she says. "This guy has it."

More tittering. The groom puts his arm around the guys flanking him.

"That's nice," Sarina says, "but why don't you make out? You're so close, you may as well. Tongue looks great in pictures. Take your shirts off."

Their grins fade. They exchange glances.

Sarina keeps snapping pictures. "You cowards. Grab each other's cocks and let's go. Jerk each other off so this is worth my while. What I'm looking at is a bunch of worthless pussies and I wanna see cock."

Ben stands behind her. "You all right?" he says.

The groomsmen jockey away from one another. "Aw, is that all you've got?" Sarina chucks the camera into the group. "Show's over, I guess." She says to Ben, "Shall we go?"

192

"Sure," Ben stammers.

They confirm the buttons and zippers of their coats, replace their hats and gloves, and leave the bar. Cabs clog the street. A sharp honk. Sarina walks ahead.

"You want to talk about that?" Ben says, trailing her.

She blinks. "Talk about what?"

12:10 A.M.

Madeleine wakes, palms and armpits damp. For a moment she does not remember the events of the day. When she does she rolls over to burrow deeper into the blankets. Her forehead flattens against the spine of a book.

History of Jazz, Volume Two.

Madeleine clutches it to her chest. Her father! She touches each picture on the cover. A phalanx of saxes. Louis Armstrong, cheeks blazing. Billie Holiday, in the ecstasy before singing. Madeleine flips each page with the care of a scientist. Toward the back she finds the write-up on The Cat's Pajamas with two (two!) pictures. She forces herself to read the entry before allowing herself a look at the pictures.

The Cat's Pajamas is a squat outcropping on Richmond Street in the city's Fishtown neighborhood. It was founded by Giuseppe Lorca in 1963, who passed it down to his son, Francis Lorca, under whose owner-ship it became a magnet for world-class acts. At one time it was the #1 jazz venue on the East Coast, hosting the likes of John Coltrane, Hampton Hawes, Bud Powell, and Horace Silver, who called the club,

"My second womb, the only place to build chops." Francis Lorca ran The Cat's Pajamas until suffering a stroke during a late-night hang, literally passing away behind the bar. He willed the club to his son, Jack. In recent days, as jazz's popularity dwindles, The Cat's Pajamas does not attract anywhere near the numbers of its heyday, though nearby jazz club Mongoose's (see pages 156–159) continues to thrive.

In a black-and-white photograph a man holds up a guitar like a prized marlin. *Francis Lorca owned one of the only known D'Angelico Snakeheads,* the caption reads. In the other photo, a woman sits at a piano, a silky black braid hanging down her back. *Every night in the 1990s Valentine Morris, a girl from the neighborhood, led a raucous hang until the wee hours of dawn.*

Madeleine covers and uncovers the woman's face with her fingertip. Valentine grins, gums showing over perfect teeth, stomping on the pedals. Madeleine can hear the jangle of this woman's laugh. She feels the faultless ivory keys, the pat of her feet on the pedals.

"A local girl," Madeleine recites. ". . . named Valentine Morris." She presses her cheek against the book's centerfold, a boozy picture of the New York skyline.

She hears scratching at the front door. She opens it and Pedro saunters in, looking bored, unaffected by the panic he has caused. He circles around himself and falls asleep on the rug.

12:15 A.M.

*T*hrough the cavities of a demolished house, Ben and Sarina can see the first few trees of Fairmount Park. A mutter of bushes.

"Does that park make you sad?" Ben says. "It makes me sad."

"It's just a park," says Sarina.

"Ornery," Ben says, "is what I would call it. Better-him-than-me kind of park. I'd bet even the animals who live in it are defensive and mean. Grumpy foxes. Depressive robins."

"Owls that are always talking about themselves," Sarina says. "Without ever asking about you."

"Put a sock in it, owl," Ben says.

Sarina's mother calls: *Sarina!*

"Should we go in?" he says. "Or, shall we continue our tour of the city's fountains?"

"Pardon?" Sarina says.

With a sweep of his hand, Ben showcases the city. "Our tour . . ."

"Sarina!" her mother yells. "He'll be here any minute!"

"I'll be right down!" Sarina bows her head in prayer. She is twenty years younger and standing in front of her bedroom mirror. She wears her grandmother's dress, whisper-soft and yellow.

197

Ben, twenty years younger, races his older brother Jeff's '65 Mustang up the road to Sarina's house. He was allowed to borrow the car only after promising to uphold several conditions spelled out while Jeff clutched his wrist so tightly the veins protruded. He will not punch the brakes, he will not throttle the gears, he will not drive over sixty-five miles per hour.

He has it up to eighty-five, gut in throat, suit jacket folded on the rumble seat beside him, underneath a yellow wrist corsage his mother picked out. Houses flash by. The meadow that borders the road is gold in grain. Perspiration coats the back of his neck. He fumbles for napkins in the glove compartment and applies them to his neck, taking each corner slowly, all windows down, so he is dry when he reaches her house.

He parks, gets out, and tucks in his shirt using the window as a mirror. He is halfway up the driveway when he realizes he forgot the corsage. He runs back to the car. He has almost reached her house again when he decides he should wear the suit jacket. Back to the car.

Sarina's mother and sister sit on the window seat, drinking tea. They watch the boy return to his car for the second time.

"The corsage," her mother said, on the first go-back.

"What is it now," her sister says, on the second. "Oh, the suit jacket."

Sarina's mother made the teacups out of found glass. She made the window seat's cushions from discarded fabric she found in a neighbor's trash. Her mother sees all objects in the world in two ways simultaneously: what they are and what they could be. She never gives up on anything, simply repurposes it. She had tailored her own mother's dress to fit Sarina's petite shape, happy that her daughter wanted to go to her prom and wear something other than black.

When it seems the boy plans to complete this trip to the house, her mother calls out: "Sarina!"

"I'm coming!" Sarina descends the stairs, careful not to catch her heels in the thick carpet. Her mother and sister sit with Ben Allen in the family room. How strange to see him in the room where she eats dinner, watches the news with her father, reads while her mother talks on the phone, or does homework. Her father had outfitted the windows with delicate lighting and low, wide sills, where she would sit and wish for a different family. Up until now she has hated this room; however the new fact of Ben in it, sitting in her father's chair, makes her understand that even it is capable of beauty. Up until he asked her to the prom, Sarina had been certain high school would hold no bright spots.

Her mother stands when Sarina enters the room. The teacup clatters on the plate. "Beautiful." Her eyes go to Ben.

"You took your piercings out," he says.

Her mother takes a few stilted photos. They walk to the car. Ben wants to tell Sarina she looks as pretty as a yellow rose but hears Jeff say, *Play it easy, man. Don't be the guy who trips all over himself.* Ben and his brother have spent hours analyzing the Pretty Girl, specifically this one, and have come up with a few guidelines. Never tell the Pretty Girl that she is pretty. You will be like every other fool. Compliment every other girl in front of her, but never her.

So instead Ben says, "Try not to slam the door." Realizing it's the first time he's spoken to her directly, he adds, "It's not my car."

They meet Georgina McGlynn, Bella Harrington, and Tom Venuto at the school's main entrance. Tom's date is the girl from Ben's Advanced Lit class. Georgie and Bella are each other's date. They wear strapless terry-cloth dresses in pink and green, respectively. Feathers clipped to their hair. Their glittered eyelids ascend when they see Sarina.

"Are you wearing makeup?" Bella says. "Where are your piercings?"

"Your dress," Georgie says. "Vintage?"

Girls, thinks Ben. Flutelike, gauze-filled, late-afternoon sunshine. Rainbow bracelets on the carpet. They use their tongues to wet their lips. Girls. They pretend to like each other. Dotting their *i*'s with hearts, arching their backs, manipulating their confusing hair with flat irons, curling irons, glisten, extra, ultra hold, hold my purse, hold me close, no duh, bubble gum, gym socks, tube socks, tubes of gloss, tube tops, purrs, pert collars, full hair, full tits, just the tip! Their sound, the upper notes of a xylophone. Their legs, downed in fur. Girls.

The one from Ben's Advanced Lit class says, "That dress is vintage. You can totally tell."

"It was my grandmother's." Sarina checks to see if Ben is listening to people compliment her, but he is accepting a flask from Tom and finalizing the plans for a concert they will attend later in the summer.

He leans into her, creating a sacramental space between them. *Finally,* Sarina thinks, *he will say something sweet to me.* "Isn't Georgie something?" he says, as if they are locker room buddies. "She is so foxy."

A hard knot pushes against Sarina's breastplate. The envy she feels for Georgie in this moment will evolve into a feeling of inadequacy the origin of which she will be unable to remember.

The gymnasium sparkles with the dresses and accessories of their classmates. The shots of whiskey have calmed Ben down. He feels like the president of the prom. His chest swells like when he finishes writing a poem, or runs a block at full speed. Ben doesn't know who Sarina hangs with. She doesn't have a group like he does. It must bother her. He has given her a ride in a classic car and a group of slick-looking cool people. He is proud of himself for helping her out and hopes her gratitude will take the form of a killer blow job. He imagines her unzipping his pants in the front seat of the Mustang. Speaking of, where is Sarina?

He finds her outside, repositioning the straps of her dress near a group of nattering lacrosse girls.

"You forgot me."

Had he perceived her wounded tone, he could have recalibrated the alignment of his tactics. However, the insight Ben needs to fix this situation is the insight he will gain after screwing it up.

Inside the gym, the DJ plays a new indie band covering an old indie band's song.

Georgie squeals. "We must, must dance!"

Ben says he doesn't dance, they know that, right? He never dances, you dance, though. They leave him, sputtering on the side.

Bella performs her version of dancing: planting her right leg and cranking her arms like a wind-up doll.

Georgie performs her version of dancing: swinging her head back and forth. Periodic exclamations of glee.

Tom Venuto's version: wagging his ass out of time, looking askance. *I might not be dancing, I might just be walking by with pep.*

The girl from Advanced Lit's version: Hop hop hop.

Sarina's version: knees bent, motioning outward and outward, shooing away the whole world.

If you were to judge the dance floor solely on merit, you might linger on Georgie, whose family's attic is stuffed with boxes of feathered masks and bedazzled headbands. Pictures of Georgie in ballet or character shoes, holding batons, hula hoops, crystalline balls, or simply one flexed hand up to the camera's flash. However, the dancer you'd watch would be Sarina Greene. She is by no one's standards talented, but it is obvious when watching her that she loves to dance.

At the end of the song, Georgie squeals, "Wasn't that the best? I am having so much, so much fun!"

Ben spends the night in earnest conversation with other girls he would never on other occasions be interested in. Party girls. Sports girls. He talks a theater girl through a rough patch of night after a song reminds her of her dead grandmother. Without notice, she kisses him. Her tongue is down his throat before he can extract himself.

Sarina sits near the back of the gym, her hope falling like a helicopter leaf, halting, not quite reaching the bottom, not quite reaching the bottom, not quite reaching the . . . She preworried for tornadoes, fistfights, drunk driving: scenarios for Ben's heroism to shine. She didn't anticipate the dull slap of being ignored.

She spoons a melted sundae she's too sad to eat and counts the minutes until she can ask to be taken home without sounding like a bitch. If he still planned to take her home. He canoodles with a theater girl at a table near the dance floor, where Georgie and Bella enact big scenes.

What will she tell her mother, who sewed every bead on the gloves she is wearing? Who said, *Try not to think of your father tonight.* No one at school knows her father is gone and Ben has nothing to do with that gray man loading suitcases into his smoking gray car in the middle of the gray night. He was a don't-say-anything-that-takes-more-than-four-words kind of father. When looking at the world, he saw only how it was. Whatever he saw when he looked at Sarina and her mother and sister, he didn't think he needed.

Sarina had hoped for an exchange with the universe: a good prom for a gone father. But she will receive no coupon. Drab girls named Sara have as much chance for divinity. This realization sucks, brick by brick, ascending into a wall inside her that will from this day forward allow her smile to open only so big. She is not special or pretty or chosen or royal. She is fatherless, only.

Boys. Tender with their cars. Feet that smell like churned earth. Sparse bureau tops, loose change, and a dry-cleaning ticket. Dirty jeans, sun-faded socks. Upsetting smirks. Forearms dusted with freckles. Limbs long with no effort. They pretend to not care how they look. Her father's shelf in the medicine cabinet was empty except for a roll of bandages and a comb that smelled like firewood. Boys. In packs at the edges of fields, hitting each other over some new level of video game, obscure band, skate trick, lit crit, rebound, offsides, descending line, whammy bar, pickup, layup, Walkman, eight-track, on the bench, down the line, over the shirt, under the bra, fumbling toward the clit. Boys.

Another suited jerk stops in front of her table. "Sarina?" it says.

It's Michael Lawrence, the scrawny guy who sings in the school's musicals. He takes several steps as if forced back by her beauty. "You are stunning. Jean Seberg, if she was a brunette."

"I've never heard of that actress," she says.

"Jean Seberg. From *Breathless*?"

How nice to have another boy treat her like a worthless thing, this time for not knowing a movie. Then he is wrenching her from her chair, does she not want to dance? Sarina doesn't want to dance, no she can't explain why, well then, let's dance, you and me, oh Michael, oh, fine. Sarina rests her hands on his shoulders. They take one stiff step to the right, one stiff step to the left.

Across the room, Ben watches his date dance with Michael Lawrence, the human equivalent of not playing it cool. The song is about not understanding the person you're with even after all these years and even after being given every opportunity. It lasts for three minutes and fifty-three seconds. Over the course of it, Sarina and Michael cover one square foot of gym floor.

Ben, however, travels to hell and back.

The song finishes and Sarina thanks Michael for what will be her only dance. Next to her, someone clears his throat and for the first time that night, Sarina turns to find her date by her side.

"I'll take it from here," Ben says.

The smile Sarina extended to Michael dies. "You can take me home."

Ben goes numb. Any thought she might be joking fades as he trails her through the parking lot to the Mustang. She gets in and shuts the door. He gets in and shuts his, sealing out noise from the outside. On another day that would be considered another killer feature of this car, but now the silence makes Ben's suit feel a size too small. He suggests waffles at the diner.

"No," she says.

The shape of his error grows and sharpens, causing his throat to close, his stomach to leaden. He cannot let her go home. He must rebound. Rally to overturn the momentum. He puts his mouth on her earlobe, sliding his hand under the strap of her dress. She forces him away. "Home."

The Mustang rumbles to life. Ben is too upset to appreciate it.

Driving out of the parking lot, they pass the

open doors of the gym, where a couple necks underneath wilting balloons. The boy bites the girl's shoulder while she stares at the ceiling. The balloons are black and gray, in coordination with the prom theme: Goth Night. Ben glances over to see if Sarina is watching too, but she is staring at the soccer field that in the fall is dotted with the banners of rival schools. Ben eases around each corner, so as not to further upset her. Her neck glows like the mussel shells his family collects on shore vacations. When they reach her street, it is quiet and carless. The Mustang shudders to a halt in front of her house.

Through the bay window, Sarina can see her mother napping on the recliner. The creak of the front door will awaken her and she will want to know everything: how the dress went over, what the other girls were wearing, how it was to dance with him, whether summer picnics will include him. Her mother will want to know whether in a world of unreliable fathers this boy is going to stick. How will Sarina tell her no?

Sarina's hand pauses on the car door. She needs to gather herself into a girl who can lie, *It was great!* This terrible boy would not understand. After ignoring her all night he can at least allow her this time, unexplained. Around her the chirruping bugs, the dilations of stars, the smell of the rosebushes, even the arrogant moon seem to pause.

How would she have said good-bye to her father, even if he had stayed to hear it?

Sarina will move to college and tell this story at parties, her mouth spiced with alcohol. What was the name of that guy who did that thing? her girlfriends will say. At your prom? She will take a bong hit and yell: *Ben Allen!* in smoke. She will meet and marry a gorgeous man whose first language is Spanish. Finally—restitution from the universe. They will have sex on unpronounceable beaches. They will move to Connecticut where nothing has edges. One day, her sister will call and say come back, Mom's dying, and Sarina will drag what's left of this home to this curb in boxes they bought at the Shop and Save. In that moment, she will have gone far enough to measure how little progress she has made.

In this moment, through the bay windows and over the wide sills, Sarina watches the woman in forty-watt light readjust her chin in sleep. Ben Allen watches, too.

She says, "That's my mother."

12:30 A.M.

Alex is outfitted in the uniform of a former Cubanista twice his size: lapel-less band jacket and pants the color of whole wheat, accented with pink sequins. The excess waistband sags below his hips. He has finessed his curls away from his face with Max's hair grease, but they refuse to stay. They fall into his eyes as he huddles with Max onstage.

"Check out Tito Puente," Sonny says. He and Lorca stand behind the bar, arms crossed.

Lorca trains his eye on the front door where, he worries, a fleet of cops led by Len Thomas will burst through any moment. "Probably a bad idea letting him play."

"Everything is a bad idea," Sonny says.

Max swills water at the bar. "No hazing," Lorca tells him. "Don't make him scuffle for chord changes."

"That's how you learn, buddy." Max cha-cha-chas for the ladies and goes back onstage.

Alex likes to be close to the percussion when he plays. He takes the chair next to Gus and vaults his brunette guitar onto his knee. He noodles, alert as a puppy, as Max rains more love on the girl in yellow heels. Max explains in his thick baritone what she should listen for as he plays, why each note is important.

"Got it," she says, irritated.

"Let's go, Max." Sonny yells through his cupped hands. Then he says to Lorca, "They look like a loaf of bread."

Max cannot see Sonny through the stage's glare when he purrs into the microphone, "Suck it, Vega, we go when we're ready," accenting the insult with a low kick. A cymbal hit by Gus. Max croons, "Ladies and gentlemen, we are the Cubanistas and we have come all the way from Cuba to play for you tonight."

Cassidy snorts, pouring a pint.

"We would like to start with a *classique de la Cubanista*. It is called 'Candela.' We do hope you enjoy it."

The Main Line kid hisses some important distraction into Aruna's ear, but she swats him away. Her gaze is trained on Alex, who pats his wet forehead with the back of his wrist.

Max hits the first chord and bays to the ceiling, silencing the people who enter, shaking off the cold. The other musicians join. At first, they keep pace with each other, laying their rhythms over Gus's timbales. Max rolls his shoulders in time. He calls out to the tin roof. In the space of one note, he sings three. He warbles up the ascending line. Hearing him sing is observing someone in great pain. He's not reliable or even predictable.

He'll lead a song off a cliff if it means checking out a sound lurking in the valley. Lorca has heard him drift so far he forgets what song he's playing, but he can make even venerable horn players turn.

Max howls, gargles tri-notes, making everyone in the audience feel they are in on something. Windmills, thrusts, beads of sweat on the crab apples of his cheeks. He chugs almost offstage, then stalks back to keen Spanish into the mic. Max could reason with the archangel on Judgment Day, or just a university girl out of her dress. He stays drunk, scared of the part of himself that is able to blow his mind so far out. If he ever got sober, he'd be chatty and nervous, no better than the bums in the square playing chess with the pigeons, telling them he used to be a jazz great, and the pigeons would say, *The hell you were, Max. Checkmate.* Lorca knows so much of Max is bullshit. But when it comes to playing, he is the genuine article and has spent his life in service. For Alex to keep pace, he will have to adjust to quick-shifting harmonies and note patterns.

Emo Sonofabitch Gladden solos. How he plays the trumpet: like a son of a bitch. His fingers are thick as garden carrots, but deft. He blows a phrase and it sounds like a girl saying, "come here."

It is almost time for Alex's solo. Lorca strums his son's chords on his jeans. He wants to play it for him, but he can only watch.

The song surges into a different tempo. Alex pauses on the edge like a Northeast girl waiting to jump into double-Dutch, searching for the right height, or some incalculable readying of sound. Max calls out that this is his party and he loves to sing. The ropes go over and under and over and under.

Alex chases after a few notes, but they don't please him. He hunts for a run he likes more. Gus's percussion supports him as he noodles. Alex listens for chords in the strings, his eyes at a fixed point over the crowd. He finds it. He lands it again. The people at the front tables stop talking. Holding silver-rimmed liquor bottles to the mouth of a drink, Cassidy stops talking. Even Max, spraying saliva into the microphone, nods. The song collects behind Alex's lead. He licks at something sparkling at the corner of his mouth. He takes a run, picks at a particular line, threads it, *yes* he says because he likes it, holds it, noses into it, asks if it has anything more, lets it go.

Lorca exhales. He guesses where his son will leap and is wrong every time. *Can't catch me,* Alex's tempos seem to say before leaping in wild directions. He's better than this club already, it's all over his posture, more like that of a visiting musician stopping off on his way somewhere better. An urge cracks beneath Lorca's breastplate. He wants to be softer with Alex, encourage this tender talent. This is how it must feel to be a good father. But then the urge is replaced by helplessness; the amount of energy it would take to reverse the father he already has going would be too much. He can't be expected to do that plus operate a club. If Alex keeps playing, all he'll have are these balding nights with strangers. He'll be surrounded by people like him, Max, and Sonny. This is no life. Who does Alex think he is? Lorca is filled by a quick, cheap anger. Alex has made it impossible to father him. Then this feeling too parts and is replaced. Lorca is tired of trying to keep the club together. The keg orders, the rotting basement, the floors that cling to their stains. Lorca wants to sit in a boat with no task more urgent than finding a fish with bait. He slumps next to Sonny at the bar, weary from this rearrangement of disposition, though only a short time has passed, the time it takes Alex to reposition his guitar, bringing the neck within breath's distance so he has easier access to its strings.

Max yells, rolls. The song builds to one repeating line that Alex solos over.

"I'm burning," Max sings. "I'm burning, I'm burning."

Alex's notes go under and over and under and over.

"Look everyone," the Cubanistas sing, "he's burning."

It's up to Alex to gather the whole mess like a

family: Max's baying, Gus's percussion, Emo's snivelly, choppy horn. But he's having too much fun.

"I'm burning," Max yells.

"He's burning," the Cubanistas sing.

Alex lands the final chord and releases the room. The club goes blank with noise. The crowd can't get to their feet fast enough. They yell through megaphones they construct from their hands. Max applauds himself, the band, and Alex.

"Not too shabby," he says into the microphone, forgetting his accent.

Alex kneads sweat into the denim of his thigh. He blinks toward where his father is, though he cannot see him through the gluten of bodies.

Sonny whistles and stomps. "Good job, Dad," he says to Lorca.

A young girl looks up. "Are you his dad?"

"He sure is, darling." Sonny beams.

"Does he have . . ." Her friends close ranks around her. One of them finishes her question. ". . . a girlfriend?"

Three pairs of eyes lined in charcoal wait for Lorca to answer. The muscles in his back tense with pride. "Single as a bluebird," he says.

Onstage, Alex is being tousled and hugged by the Cubanistas. Max makes a show of fending off the audience. Alex is congratulated to the bar, where the trio of girls bluff errands in their purses, fuzz on their stockings.

214

"Drink?" Cassidy says.

"Whiskey, please." He turns to his father. His eyes are slick. "How'd I do, Pop?"

Lorca doesn't answer.

"Pop?"

"You were great, kid." Sonny pounds his shoulders. But Alex wants to hear it from his father.

"You showboated behind Emo's solo," Lorca says. "You should have been supporting him, letting him take the chances."

Sonny winces. "Come on, Lorc."

"May we please have the little guitarist back onstage?" Max hums into the microphone. "*Leetle* guitarist?"

Alex gets his whiskey and goes back onstage, no longer smiling.

Three pairs of charcoal eyes scrutinize Lorca. "Damn," says the first girl. "I wouldn't want to be your son."

12:42 A.M.

It gets TOAD away!" Sarina exclaims, before he can answer. Ben's mouth contorts, trying not to laugh.

12:41 A.M.

Sarina's face is serious. "For example," she says. "What happens when a frog's car breaks down?"

Ben taps his foot against the bleacher, thinking.

"Give up?" she says.

He throws out his hands in phony exasperation. "Give a man some time to think."

12:40 A.M.

"Can you do better?" Ben says.

"In my sleep, fella. I've got jokes for days."

12:39 A.M.

Ben and Sarina sit on bleachers at the baseball field on Chestnut. A mural of autumn trees stretches over the entire wall of a row home across

216

the street. Their clothes are almost dry. "This public art is getting out of hand," Sarina says.

"Did you hear the one about the two leaves?" Ben says. "Sitting on a branch together? One leaf turns to the other and says, 'It's really windy.' And the other leaf says, 'Help, a talking leaf!'"

Sarina rolls her eyes. "Major groan."

12:43 A.M.

A breeze bickers around the bleachers. Sarina hugs her coat tighter. "What time do you think it is?"

"It could be eleven or three and I'd believe it." Ben consults his watch. "Twelve forty-three."

She asks if he wants to talk about it. He doesn't answer. A cab slows in front of them. Its driver calls, "You two want a ride?"

Ben waves. "We're fine, thanks."

The cabdriver regards them with longing. "Olde City? Northern Liberties? Ten dollars."

"Christian Street," Ben says.

"Five dollars."

Sarina's feet ache, but a cab ride will end their night sooner than she wants. "It's late," she says, hoping he'll protest. "Maybe I should go home."

"Can you do two stops?" Ben asks the cabbie.

"I can do anything."

"Deal." Ben says. He climbs in and Sarina, disappointed, follows. The cab is lit by strands of jalapeño and twinkle lights.

"So glad," the cabbie says. "I was about to fall asleep. You two just married?"

"Why would you guess that?" Sarina is pleased.

The cabbie's face glows red then green. "Friendly talk."

"Not married," Ben says.

He answered fast, she thinks. It wouldn't be hell, being married to her. She knows some things about some things.

"I get it," the cabbie says. "Won't commit. Wants to go to the club with her girlfriends. Doesn't want to be wired to some guy day and night."

"You got that right, bud," Sarina says. "Life is short."

"Call me Martin."

"Life is short, Martin."

Ben shakes his head. "Infuriating. Going to the club day and night with her girlfriends."

"Snorting blow," the cabbie offers, watching them in the rearview mirror.

"Mountains of it," Sarina says.

"Guys' phone numbers falling out of her pockets like rain," Ben says.

"Like a hurricane," the cabbie says. "Like that one we had last year. You guys around for that?"

"My car flooded," Ben says.

They drive in silence. Sarina watches the boarded-up market flash by.

After a while, Ben speaks. "She won't let me tell anyone. She's worried what everyone will think. Who's everyone, I keep saying."

"The Joneses," Sarina says.

"Exactly. Everyone is everyone. She said if we divorce, I won't get any of her money."

"Well, you didn't marry her for money."

"I did not."

A bus glides toward the jazz clubs on Girard. "Why did you marry her?"

"I married her," Ben says, "because I thought she was a nice person. That we would have a nice life." The cab clatters over a pothole. "Turns out, she's not that nice."

Martin drums on the steering wheel. "You want to see me do the expressway with no hands?"

"I'm a big fan of driving with hands," Ben says.

"You're no fun. I can see why she won't marry you."

"I'm a lawyer," Ben says, by way of explanation.

"Don't curse at me, buddy."

"He's a writer," Sarina says.

"Cockle-doodle-doo," says Martin. "A writer."

"That's right," Sarina says. "Cluck cluck. Now, turn on this street, count to three, then stop 'cause we're there."

Martin brakes at the archway leading to Sarina's horseshoe-shaped building. The whiskey has made her optimistic. She smells baking cookies. It is Christmas Eve Eve and she doesn't have to work tomorrow. No matter what happens she has already had a good night. She points to her courtyard, where a waterless fountain loiters, producing nothing. "Do you see what I see?"

"Oho," Ben says.

"Race you?"

"Lady, you have no idea what you're in—"

She takes off. He chases her into the courtyard. She is winning then he is winning then she is winning. He grabs for the strap of her bag. She lunges for his scarf. It is an urgent, silly display. He leaps the wall and is inside the fountain. One of her heels has come off in the race. She hops on one foot while throwing the other heel off.

"The winner!" he cries.

Sarina feigns dramatic, faltering loss. Ben feigns accepting bouquets from an audience. She feigns cutting her own throat in agony. He feigns running to her: resuscitation. She feigns death. He feigns imploring heaven for answers. Receiving none, he stabs himself in the chest. Then they are both dead.

"Good luck," Martin, tired of waiting, calls out as he drives away.

Sarina and Ben watch him leave from the fountain. "Martin!" Ben says. "You traitor."

"I think saying good luck to someone is the meanest thing," Sarina says. "I'll call you a cab. You suck at dying."

From one of the apartments above them, a Frank Sinatra song. They help each other up. Their breath in the fountain.

"Where is that coming from?" Ben's eyes are bright. "Should we dance?"

Sarina puts her hands at twelve and three, like Madame Jennings instructs her children to do at

Saint Anthony's. "Donce?" she says, performing a deep plié.

"Dance." Ben encircles her with one arm.

Sarina rests her chin on his shoulder. All of this is between his hand and her bare skin: her thick coat, blouse, camisole, black lace bra, citrus lotion.

The song keeps going. The courtyard smells like bike grease and Ben's skin. He holds her hand in his gloved hand. There is no wind. Ta tum, ta tum, Ben sings into her ear. Ta tum.

Several streets away, Martin slows at a stop sign. Over an abandoned lot, the PSFS building looms. An elevator climbs its spine. The lot is filled with old bar signs and truck parts. Martin lets out a low whistle. "Get a load of that pretty city."

The song comes to an end and a faster one begins.

Ben releases Sarina and performs a wild one-two-three he hopes will make her laugh. But the neighbors rethink music; it ceases with an unceremonious click. A television turns on.

"I guess that's it," he says.

On her porch, Sarina roots in her bag for her keys. The dirty light from her neighbor's porch makes everyone on hers seem shoddy.

Ben's mind is peaceful and blank. The whiskey has made his jaw feel achy and sparkly, as if he has blown up a balloon.

If she asks him to come in, he will say no. To ask to come in would not only acknowledge but cross the line they have been skirting all night. Since he cannot ask to come in or accept any invitation to do so, he wants the whole thing to be over. He yearns to leave so he can think about her. He will buy himself a pear at one of the twenty-four-hour places so he has something to toss to himself as he walks. He will reference the hand that held her like an important emissary. In his mind, he is already crossing the courtyard. He is buying the pear. He is saying to the vendor, "Love pears. Red Anjou, green Anjou, An Jou-st don't care."

Find your keys, Sarina.

He can no longer stand on this porch in agony. He can no longer sit in that car, on the night of that dance when he did everything wrong. He heard a few days later that her father had left her family, so on prom night she had been newly abandoned. How many girls did he take out in college and law school to atone? How many relationships did he solidify, even when his investment was weak to wavering?

"Do you want to come in? I make a killer martini." She cringes. She is not the kind of girl who calls martinis killer.

"I can't." He sounds early for his cue. "Busy day tomorrow."

"I found them!" She jangles her keys.

"At last."

"There is something I want to say." It's a lie. She only wants to keep him here, on her porch, for another moment.

"Anything." He worries she will say something that will drag the night's meaning into full view. He worries even more that she won't. Her neighbor's television is loud enough to hear that it is a rebroadcast of the game, but not loud enough to hear the score.

"I forget what I wanted to say."

"I'll wait."

"You might be here a while," she says. "My memory is worse than a goldfish's."

He pauses in the yellow light. "No hurry."

There is rustling next to them, the sound of a window being thrown open. A girl wearing a Santa hat and a clothespin on her nose climbs out. "Miss Greene?" she says, as if standing in front of a deep forest, calling out for anyone she knows.

Sarina's jaw slackens with surprise. "Madeleine?"

1:00 A.M.

After their wedding, Ben and Annie buy a town house in Olde City and protect it with a top-of-the-line security system. Every night, Annie smooths moisturizer into her elbows and lists the following day's To Do items. Depositions, recycling, the post office. Ben watches her as if from the other side of a bay. Who is this tall, freckled woman and why has he done something as important as marriage to her? He makes excuses to linger in his home office, tapping at his manuscript. She seems relieved. The sexless weeks pile up.

He tries coming at her from behind, in the shower, like a predatory fish. This dissolves into polite intercourse. He moves into her as if he doesn't wish to disturb her. Any interruption, a loud commercial or a passing siren, derails their tenuous physicality and they fall asleep, separate and worried.

Every time they leave their town house, they punch the security code into a panel by the door and when they return, same code.

Ben blames his job. He decides to quit to try writing full-time. She resents the extra burden placed on her salary and discusses their problems loudly on the phone to her girlfriends. "He's not a sexual person, is all," she tells them, toeing one battered, elegant slipper. "Most men like sex. This one doesn't."

Her supple elbows. Her pale, elegant neck. He cannot imagine ever wanting to fuck her again. One night, sleeping on the couch, he jolts awake to find her standing at the foot. "There's only one thing to be done," she says.

Their relationship had been careening toward it the entire time, he realizes, like the inevitable shoe drop of death.

During their first salsa lesson, the instructor explains that Cuban salsa moves on the one, and that the clave, "Cuba's answer to the cowbell," will guide them. Instead of Annie, Ben is paired with Rue, the assistant, who has forgotten to get old. Her laugh is easy, her ass taut. She leads him through the moves whose Spanish terms translate roughly into misogynist commands: Give me the girl! Tell her no! Ben immediately takes to the simple "Coca Cola," where he releases Rue for a beat before winding her back. "Date her cousin!" the instructor barks as they flop across the floor. "Plug her in!" Ben focuses on finding and maintaining the one, as across the room, Annie coca colas fearfully with her own partner, a tax attorney whose blinking face seems overexposed, like it is missing a pair of glasses. He treads on her toe and Annie giggles, looking for a moment like the young, sick girl Ben met outside Ethics of

226

Law. That night, they return home, sweaty and hopeful. *You liked it, didn't you? It wasn't bad at all.* Perhaps the chance to rekindle comes around as often as the one, Ben thinks, if you listen for it.

Wednesday night becomes salsa night. Ben likes how the students say encouraging things to one another when it is their turn to cross the floor. He likes the tax attorney's contented grimace when he accomplishes a new move. He likes that everyone laughs at one another's jokes, even when they aren't funny, because it isn't about being clever, it's about being present. He likes the idea of working on his dance phrasing, that everyone has a dance floor persona. Clara hits heavy on the floor, while Rue is airier, like a responsive, silk curtain. He likes that dance is a conversation, conducted in pressings made through the hands or against the small of his partner's back.

One night, the unthinkable happens. Ben tells her no at the right time and forgets to panic. This combination triggers a feeling of well-being as he and Rue cross the floor. Within rhythm are spaces large enough for experimentation, he realizes. He enters those spaces with his body. He dates her cousin, and it works. Rue, sensing the window that has been created by Ben's new ease, performs a butt twitch that sends a start through his pelvis. They slap the floor with their feet, they take preening, buoyant stances. Everything they attempt succeeds. They finish, laminated in sweat. The class thrills and cheers.

Why, Ben thinks, panting and frozen in his final pose, would dancing be something you'd ever do with your wife?

After class, stabbing the code into the security system, Annie ticks off insults against Rue and the class. She accuses him of faking his initial hesitance to force her into looking like a fool. She tosses a blanket and pillow at him and Ben takes his place on the couch.

The next morning, crisp and pressed, Annie informs him that salsa is boring and not helping. They will quit the class and make an appointment with a couples therapist.

Ben finds himself in the unexpected position of being devastated. He begins to sneak out. Walking home from one of these clandestine lessons, toweling off telltale sweat, he imagines cradling the small of Sarina Greene's back and, over and over, guiding her to the floor.

The little girl's diminutive stature does not match her world-weary voice. Sarina updates Ben under her breath: this is the girl she told him about with the singing and the apples and the head lice. Ben is drunk and loves and trusts this whirling coincidental night. Of course, why shouldn't they meet the girl from the story? What else can this night put forth? In advance, he accepts!

"I live here," the little girl tells Sarina, pointing to her house. "I live right here."

Sarina uses what must be her teaching tone. "Go back to bed," she says. "I will apologize to your father in the morning."

"A freight train couldn't wake him up. Who's that?"

"My friend Ben."

Ben holds out his hand. "How do you do."

Her face is blotchy with sleep. Her clothes are wrinkled and old looking. "Madeleine," she says. "Charmed."

"And what is it that you do?" he flirts. "Do you sell real estate? Do you preside over family court?" Ben can tell when he's winning someone by the corners of their mouth. One side normally relents first. This girl's mouth keeps its downward shape.

"I'm a student at Saint Anthony's grade school. Or, I was. I got expelled today."

"So, you spend your days student-ing."

"This is not the girl," Sarina whispers. Ben can tell it's a warning, but he is in a different part of the city with Sarina and a strange girl and he has done more in one night than he has in two years.

"Would you like to see a magic trick?" he says. "I can make this whole courtyard disappear."

"Do it then." Madeleine has the bluntness of a

city girl. She will watch a magic trick, but it had better be good.

"I'll need a few things. Your sweater. Off."

"My sweater?" Sarina says. "Why?"

"You girls ask a lot of questions."

Sarina removes her sweater, revealing the shell of her blouse for an instant before it is covered by her coat. Ben takes his time folding it onto the ground in front of the little girl. He moves one hand over it as if stirring a cauldron. "Before we begin," he says, "take in the courtyard around you. What do you see? Bikes, stacks of newspapers, the fountain, your front door, everyone else's front door, the window boxes, the bikes, the street through the arch." The girl obliges, looks around. "Your cares, your sorrows. All of those things are about to be gone. Are you prepared?"

"Do it already."

"Don't rush me, little girl." He conjures the sweater. "Count to seven."

"Don't you mean three?" she says.

"Who has time to do anything in three seconds?" The girl still doesn't laugh.

"One . . ." he begins.

". . . two," she says.

"Threefourfive," helps Sarina.

"Six," the girl decides. "And seven."

Ben flips the sweater up into the air and covers the girl's face.

"Presto! The courtyard has vanished."

"This is bullshit," the girl says, underneath the sweater.

"Language," Sarina says, helping to free her.

"You do something then," Ben says. "And don't try to sell me a duplex because I already have one."

The girl smooths her eyebrows and skirt. "I sing."

Sarina's breath catches in her throat. "I've never heard you sing."

"Do it!" Ben says. "You can't say you can sing and then not sing. It's like saying you can sing and then not singing."

The girl searches his face for something that tells her whether he is worth it. Ben is accustomed to this look. It is normally followed by the slam of a bedroom door and a night of uninterrupted History Channel. However, this little girl finds what she is looking for.

"Okay," she nods.

He is surprised by how much this pleases him. "Back up!" he announces. He positions Sarina on the bottom step. He attempts to lean against the pillar but his foot finds no ground. He has forgotten the two steps leading up to the porch. He falls up. One leg vaults out in front of him; the other, bent at the knee, follows. Unsupported by either leg, arms thrown back toward Sarina's door, he forms a four-pointed star in the air. He lands gracelessly, elbow hitting the hard steps before the back of his head, calves, ass. He sees white then gray then white. In the air hangs the smell of wet roses, but that can't be, it's the wrong season. Sarina is behind a thick pane of glass cheering for him as he swims underwater. What is she saying? She cheers: *Ben! Ben!* He wants to answer but his mouth is filled with tin and chalk. He manages a sitting position on the ground, gravel sticking to his palms. "Give me a minute. I think I need to do this." He places his head between his knees.

"Your hand is bleeding." Sarina encircles his wrist and shows him his own injury. "I'm getting a towel." She disappears inside her apartment.

Ben dabs at his lip. "Quite a show, huh?"

The little girl shifts from foot to foot. "I've seen worse."

"I'm sorry about the apples," he says. "And the lice. It doesn't seem fair."

"Life's not fair," she says.

"Tush," he says. "The world is much more interesting than that. Sometimes, of course, it's not fair. But sometimes it's very fair, overly fair, so fair that you want to throw up from all the fairness. Then it goes back to being unfair. The world is cyclical." He shakes a cigarette from his pack. "Do you mind?"

"Can I have one?"

"She"—he jerks a thumb toward the door—

"would throttle me." He smokes. He checks; Sarina is still inside. "One drag."

The girl inhales and hands the cigarette back. "Do you know about The Cat's Pajamas?"

This is what Sarina passes as she hurries toward the kitchen: a sofa with stray glitter collected in its folds, a smattering of Popsicle sticks, a CD of songs with the word *home* in them, a guide to making killer martinis, dark chocolate, darker chocolate, a life-size model of a heart, and an almost-finished painting on her easel. In it a man strides halfway out the front door of a common-looking family room. The viewer cannot see his face: his attention is turned toward a farther room where a boy lurks in a doorway. Half of the man's head is flayed, the skin collected in uniform curlicues at the base of his neck. The elements of his brain, each lobe and gland, are rendered in meticulous detail. His neck and arms are whole, but his torso is also stripped, revealing the heart's tender ventricles. They tumble out of the body and wind around the bank of tulips on the porch, reach toward the boy. Other canvases stacked against the wall depict similar scenes of people and animals whose interior workings are on display. An older couple walks a transparent dog in the park. An excoriated bus driver turns the enormous, flat wheel of a bus.

Sarina dampens a dish towel and trills past everything again on her way outside, where Ben sits smoking on the step that tried to delete him. She helps him arrange the ice cubes around his elbow. "I think you should go inside, Madeleine. I will see you in school next week."

"No," Madeleine says. "You won't."

"I'm sorry, but we can talk in the morning."

"Fine." Madeleine hoists one leg over the windowsill then the other. "Later, skaters." The sash snaps shut.

"Your neighborhood is much more exciting than mine," Ben says. They sit on the stoop. Sarina imagines millions of white blood cells attending to Ben's elbow, repairing thin tissue with screws and glue. "I want to dance," she admits.

"There is a place," Ben says. "It's very special. It's called The Cat's Pajamas."

Sarina laughs. "You want to DONCE with Marcos?"

"Why not?"

"How's your bleeding?"

Ben holds his wrist to his ear as if checking a watch. "How are you doing, bleeding?" He waits for an answer. "Stopped," he says. "Ready to walk."

Behind her curtains, Madeleine eavesdrops. She hears Miss Greene and Ben say they will go to The Cat's Pajamas. This starts the engine of her heart. It triple-time steps, heel drop, hit. Pas de bourrée. Pas de bourrée.

Madeleine watches them arrange their coats

and scarves, getting ready to leave. She weighs several options in the time it takes to cinch a knot.

She could open the window and scream: *Take me with you!*

She could do nothing.

She could follow them.

She could unload a sleeve of crackers into her mouth.

A voice in her mind says: *Junk that jazz book, go to bed, get your GED, marry early, have a child. Bury your useless pipes inside you in a box labeled:* never open. *Everyone will say, what a wise and rational girl you turned out to be. So different from your nutso mother.*

Madeleine closes her eyes and plucks a random card from her mother's recipe box.

DO WHAT SCARES YOU.

She flips it over. On the other side, her mother has printed: BRING A SCARF.

Miss Greene and Ben have disappeared beyond the archway. Madeleine wraps her scarf and coat around her, throws open the sash, and with a final look back into the warm square of her bedroom, clears the sill in one leap.

1:20 A.M.

*I*t has been quite a fucking day for Ted Stempel, and it's not over yet. His girlfriend has advised him she will be arriving at the store within minutes and when she does, he'd better be ready to explain. The fact that her first name is Delilah makes her last name unnecessary.

Today, Ted was supposed to help transition Delilah's grandmother from one nursing home to another. It would have required packing up the old woman's knickknacks and unmentionables at the first home, along with paperwork, niceties, maneuvering the dazed woman down the corridor into his car, taking care that none of her sagging limbs got caught in the seat belt, a ten-minute ride to the new home where, Delilah says, they don't let you sit in your own filth all day, more paperwork, niceties, knickknacks arranged on a new bureau.

Only, Ted Stempel doesn't do any of that. He tells Delilah he must work all day at the store, open twenty-four hours and owned by his wife, Kendra, who is famous for her ability to make gravy out of, like, nothing. He sleeps until noon, then walks his true love, Malcolm, a broad-shouldered pit bull puppy who has never once asked Ted to explain himself. Walking a pit bull has the surprising effect of eliminating Ted's need to engage in niceties. This is one of many reasons Ted would for Malcolm take a Louisville Slugger to the balls.

Here is Ted on South Street around three P.M., holding an extra-large hot chocolate. His brilliant boy struts next to him in his best sweater, the color of grass. Every so often, Malcolm peers up the leash to confirm that Ted is still there. Ted asks Malcolm if he is in fact the most handsome dog in the world and, without waiting for the dog's reply, assures him that yes, he is. Ted admires a window display that showcases a new Harley-Davidson and imagines motoring down the California coast wearing mirrored sunglasses. Daydreaming, he doesn't see the Rottweiler a block away ridding itself of its leash and barreling toward them. Ted feels an upsetting jolt at his side as the Rottweiler clamps down on Malcolm's neck and lifts him above the ground.

The young blond dog owner, screaming. A horrified parade of passersby. Ted, blinking, tries to understand the scene in front of him, as Malcolm is tossed back and forth in his perfect sweater.

The Rottweiler ignores its name, which is, improbably, Grace. The blond owner cannot get Grace to let go, and Ted cannot wrench Malcolm out of her jaws. Suddenly Grace pauses. Her owner and Ted pause, too. Malcolm, petrified, searches for Ted. *Who is this, why is this happening to me?*

"Someone," Ted chokes, "help."

A police officer arrives. He takes one tentative step toward the two-dog tableau, then another, crooning promises and compliments. His hand is poised on his holster. To his aggravation, the crowd begins to make suggestions.

"You can't pull a dog from a dog," someone says.

"Don't you think I know that?" the officer says.

Grace the Rottweiler's eyes flick from her owner to the officer. She raises Malcolm to the uppermost point of her flinging trajectory, then pauses again, as if to test her control over the scene.

"Drop it, Grace?" her owner says.

Malcolm yowls. Scared by the sound, Grace begins thrashing again. Her teeth gnash through Malcolm's sweater. Her muzzle darkens with blood. The officer raises his gun and fires once into the sky. Grace, startled, releases her hold on Malcolm, who falls to the sidewalk. The officer scoops up the pit bull and Grace is immediately captured by her owner.

A woman arrives with salves and bandages that she applies to Malcolm on the sidewalk. She is a vet or a bandage supplier, Ted fades in and out of understanding, she had been walking by . . .

"His name is Malcolm." Ted holds the bridge of his nose as tears course down his cheeks.

The woman places Malcolm into his arms. "He's scared, but he's fine."

Malcolm, from the sea of cotton bandages, looks at him with a mixture of fear and (it cannot be) adoration.

Cradling the dog to his chest, Ted walks home. He spends the day with Malcolm on his lap, reading aloud to him, changing his dressings, encouraging him to eat. When it is time for his shift he brings Malcolm to the store and arranges his bed behind the counter. He cooks a batch of his famous meatballs. The store fills with their sweet, earthy smell. It is midnight when his cell phone vibrates in the pocket of his jeans. Delilah. He wants to tell her that he has experienced a universal near miss. He wants her to say Malcolm will be recovered in no time.

Instead, Delilah goes first. "Do you want to tell me how you were on South Street today talking to some dumb bitch when you were supposed to be working? She saw you. Gina saw you on South Street."

"Gina?" Ted says.

"I am coming there after my shift and you'd better be ready to explain how when you were at work you were also in Center City talking to some dumb bitch."

Ted hangs up the phone. A couple enters the store and surveys the produce. He checks on Malcolm, who has been asleep for the past hour, head nestled between his marshmallow paws.

When Delilah arrives, Ted will tell her that they will never again be naked and clasped at the middle, thrusting toward her signed poster of Shane Victorino. He will never again have to use her cheap, cotton candy soap. He will never again have to deal with her accent: the tinned *a*'s, the sour *o*'s, the spine-splitting sound of *l*'s pronounced as *w*'s. Gina *sawl* you on South Street.

This decision fills Ted Stempel with a happy, reasonable light.

When the couple reaches the counter, he responds to the woman's smile with an even bigger one.

"How are we tonight?" He rings the man up for his pears.

"Look at that adorable dog." The woman cranes her neck over the counter. "What's his name?"

"Malcolm," says Ted.

"If I had a dog that cute, I'd take him to work with me, too," the woman says.

"He's got bandages on," says the man. "Is he okay?"

Ted swells with pride. "He's a champion. On second thought." He voids the transaction. "The pears are free."

240

"Really?" the man says.

"Free pear night," Ted says. "Everyone gets free pears." He hands the money back to the man.

"How nice of you," the woman says. Then, to Malcolm, "See you later, alligator."

Ted replies for him. "After a while, crocodile."

"Is there anything as satisfying as a pear?" Ben says, when they are back on the street.

"Yes," Sarina says, "but you can't eat it and walk."

Ben's eyebrows ascend. He always forgets that she is funny. That underneath her traditional exterior is the girl who wore only black in high school. "Pardon me, Miss Greene?"

Sarina's cheeks turn the color of ham.

They walk and eat their pears. Night allows the objects of Christian Street to hide except for where the streetlights call them out. *There you are, newspaper stand. Hello.* A discarded umbrella: *Hello.* A hydrant. A chained bike. Sarina and Ben walk in and out of these salutations. A sign on a fence promises a community garden, after several false starts, is coming. Featuring basil and daffodils. For real this time.

1:26 A.M.

Madeleine waits until Miss Greene and Ben are a block away before emerging from behind a truck. She hears her teacher's laughter unfurl like a scarf. Outside the store, produce shines. Madeleine feels around her pockets for change. Nothing. Her stomach protests. She could steal an apple. There are hundreds. She will be fast, dangerous!

Madeleine checks inside the shop, then sleeves a Rome Beauty.

"What have you got there, little girl?" a voice behind her says. It is the store's clerk. "I have had it today," he says. "With the drama."

Madeleine shakes the apple out of her sleeve. "I shouldn't have taken it."

The clerk returns it to its stack. "It's stealing."

"I know," she says. "I'm sorry. I haven't eaten since breakfast."

"You look familiar." He narrows his eyes. "Who are you?"

"Madeleine Altimari."

"Come in here." He disappears into the store. Madeleine considers escape, but she has attended too many years of Catholic school to run. She follows him. The store is unswept. Bruised canisters of tomatoes. Deflated bags of rice.

Madeleine expects to see a cockroach scurry up the walls.

Behind the counter, the clerk loads a hoagie roll with meatballs. A dog at his feet whirrs at the smell. "Not for you," the clerk says. A television hanging in the corner is tuned to a news report about a famous actress. "Do you think it will help the city's tourism to have famous people visit?" a reporter asks some yackamo in Fox Chase.

"I don't have a crystal ball." The yackamo shrugs.

Madeleine shrugs.

The clerk is satisfied with the heft and bulk of the sandwich. "You want cheese? We've got American and Swiss."

"Any Locatelli?" she says.

"That's for pasta."

Madeleine's voice is sad. "The saltiness brings out the flavor of the meat."

"You'll have to eat this one without it." He wraps the sandwich in aluminum foil and holds it out to her. "Take it," he says. He readjusts his tack when she balks. "I knew your mother."

Madeleine knows she should not take food from strangers, but also that the city is a network of her mother's promises. Hunger punches her stomach. She unwraps half of the sandwich and takes a large bite she can barely control. Her eyes move from the man to the door.

"Got somewhere to go?" he says. The phone behind the counter rings. He answers it.

Madeleine's mouth is full. "Thank you." Clutching the sandwich, she runs out of the store.

"Hey!" he calls.

On South Street, clusters of people smoke on the sidewalk. In a church that's not Saint Anthony's, a bell chimes. Madeleine catches up to Miss Greene and Ben and follows a gasp behind.

1:30 A.M.

A church bell chimes. Ben and Sarina finish their pears. They take Second until they reach the dead yards of Fishtown. "You're a good teacher," he says. "I can tell by that girl's face when she looked at you."

"She's been through the mill. Her mother died, and her father isn't the best." Sarina worries that this heavy thought will tip the ship of the night. "She has people, though," she adds, "who help."

"Like you had people." His tone is suddenly charmless. "Not me, though. I wasn't there for you."

"You were a boy, Ben."

"I was an asshole," he says.

"Way to make it about you."

"Just let me say I'm sorry, Miss Greene."

A smattering of laughter on a rooftop settles on them. The street is filled with warehouses and crack houses, jazz clubs and people having tough conversations. "You'd be surprised by how much it hurts that he didn't say good-bye." They have reached the club. Sarina's expression is a mixture of relief (she is cold) and happiness (they have made it) and pain (she has spoken about her father) when she turns to Ben.

245

"Do you know," he says, "I think about you every single day?"

"How could I know that?"

"I'm telling you."

"We're here," she says. "Let's go in."

He doesn't move. "Do you think about me?"

Bundled skinny boys, one whistling off tune, scuffle through the door into the club.

"I'm cold," Sarina says. "I forget the question."

"You do not."

"I think that you're not free. Even if you are going to be. You'll lose a year, at least. At the end of it, you'll be a different person who wants different things. I've been through it."

For the first time, Ben feels the chill anesthetizing his elbows and toes. In one of the warehouses, someone opens a window to clear a stinking room.

"What am I supposed to do," she says. "Wait?" She wants him to say, *Yes, wait. I will be home as soon as I run this one errand.* Ben perceives disgust in her tone. Why would anyone wait for him? A boy who didn't know how to be a prom date, a man who knows what he needs, but too late.

He releases her arm. His voice is professional with sorrow. "You certainly couldn't do that." He means because she is precious. Sarina hears that she is snotty and unkind. He means because he is not that lucky; she hears: he is bored.

No one says *I want you to wait* and no one says *I'll wait.*

Ben enters the club and Sarina follows. A concussion of guitar and drums pauses them. "I'm going to . . ." He points to the bar. She points to the ladies' room.

In front of the bathroom mirrors, women administer to themselves. One draws her eyebrows on. One bemoans a botched waxing. One says into her phone that she is out of here if he doesn't show. *The hoops I've jumped through,* she says, balancing the phone and washing her hands. Another woman combs and recombs her bangs. A vase of fake flowers brightens up an old bureau. Sarina slumps against it, sees herself unglossed in the mirror. She removes her coat, her sweater. She finds a compact and tube of lipstick in her bag. She takes down her hair. She puts it back up. She takes it back down.

Do you know I think about you every single day?

"Down," the woman who has jumped through hoops says to Sarina about her hair.

"You think?"

The woman stabs at her pucker with a shade of peach. "I know."

Sarina locks herself in a stall and plans. She will find him at the bar. He will be angry—drinking a scotch, neat. She will say his name and pause for the amount of time it takes to unsnap a bra, so he can process her lips, her hair, before she moves into him. She will open his mouth with hers. She will lead him through the club, into the men's room. He will lift her onto the sink's counter and slide his hands down her thighs. She will catch glimpses of him in the mirror. Her mind will be her childhood road in early morning; the breeze in the weeping willow.

Back in the club, musicians play on a blue stage. Sarina has never heard music like this. A quick guitar and a bank of drumming. Black coats and red lipstick. The crowd at the bar is three deep. The floor beneath Sarina's heels pulses.

When she finds him at the bar, Ben is talking to Marcos and a redheaded girl. The night has contained so many chasms it has achieved an echo. An overcologned reprise. *This is fucking bullshit,* Madeleine had screamed in the principal's office, and she was right.

My God, Sarina thinks, *this terrible night.*

1:35 A.M.

*T*his goose-pimply, gold star of a night!
While every other girl in the fifth grade is asleep, Madeleine is finishing a hoagie in the electric air across the street from The Cat's Pajamas, meeting place of witches and ice cream men. The club is nondescript in a row of warehouses the color of potato sacks. A gust from the river. A couple pushes through the club's doors, choking with laughter, and bounds toward Girard. Gypsies, thinks Madeleine. She crosses the street and stands in front of the club. She places her hand against the door. Wood. Her bed is made out of wood. So is her mother's recipe box. Wood is not scary. She uses both hands to open the heavy door, hears music, and slips inside. The vestibule smells like cinnamon gum. There is a stack of phone books and another door, this one quilted and red. She peeks through it for the length of a glimpse: a red room with tables and chairs, each of them filled with people. A woman sneezes. Madeleine says, "God bless you." She lets the door close and is once again a secret in the vestibule.

Two men enter from outside. One of them wears a stiff-looking suit lined in sequins. They seem to want to get to the main room as fast as they can. Madeleine tells herself—*go!* She uses their current to enter the club unseen.

Coats bulge out from an overworked rack near the door. A bar runs along the wall on her right, lit at the top by twinkle lights. The ceiling is tin with designs punched into it. At the end of the bar the room swells into the dome of a stage where a young man with a red scarf plays a guitar pointed forward on his knee. His fingers move so quickly the sound seems delayed. If anyone notices her, she will disappear like Clarence through a crack. Hidden in the coats, Madeleine's heart does the rumba.

1:40 A.M.

*T*he girl, introduced as Cassidy, can't be more than eighteen, Sarina thinks. In the crook of Marcos's elbow, she looks like a niece corralled into an affectionate hug during a family football game.

"I work here!" the girl yells. "We're going to dance!"

It is too loud to talk. Ben avoids Sarina's eyes as Cassidy says something into his ear. Sarina assumes it is a general bar request, a napkin or more ice; however, Ben slides off his stool. Holding her hand, he leads her into the crowd of people on the dance floor.

"She likes to make me jealous!" Marcos says, taking Ben's place on the stool.

"How thoughtful of her!" Sarina recrosses her legs. Ben doesn't dance, she thinks. At their prom, at every wedding they've suffered through at different tables, she doesn't remember him dancing. Sarina had to live through fifteen years of friendship to dance with him in a fountain, but this girl did it with a quick message delivered to the vicinity of his collar. No matter. It will be a clumsy display. The song is Latin, demanding passion and hips. The girl will get frustrated. People will become uncomfortable. The sprinklers will turn on.

251

The musicians sweat. The song changes without stopping to one that's more urgent. Ben and Cassidy reach the middle of the floor. Sarina takes absentminded sips of her whiskey and waits to see what they will do.

Cassidy begins a textbook salsa she returns to after spinning or completing a controlled slide. Sarina can see her bra winking from under a low-backed tank top. Par-rum-rum. Slide. Flashing gold charm near her collarbone. Par-rum-rum. Slide. Strands of hair plastered against her neck. Her gummy smile.

"She's hot, right?" Marcos says.

"Ben can't dance!" It is the only thing Sarina can think of to say that isn't a lie. Though it appears to be a lie tonight. When the girl spins, he catches her and moves his feet in time with hers. He does his own spin. He hits appropriate postures. He laughs because he is having fun.

"Sometimes it's about having the right partner!" Marcos moves his feet in time. "You look like you swallowed a rat!"

"I'm having a ball!" Sarina yells. "Your chest hair is distracting!"

He emancipates another button on his shirt. "Be a bitch!" he says.

The guitarist introduces a slow, gritty segue. The percussion simmers. Ben and the girl transition into an almost dirge: both of their arms are slack, his head buried in her neck.

Sarina removes her glasses and places them on the bar. She calls for another whiskey. An invisible god with strong hands squeezes her head. It is the senior prom again, only now she's wearing natural fibers.

Ben: Be cool. Coca cola. Be cool. What am I doing? Be cool. Coca cola. Plug her in! Step, step. Tell her no! What am I doing (missed one, catch it up, parry step ([for the love of]!) Tell her no! Everything is—plug her in! Everything is. Step, step. What am I doing, think about it, date her cousin, mix it up and don't get boring (this girl smells like Comet cleanser)—pelvis jut! Coca cola. Pelvis jut! Everything is. Comet cleanser. Tell her no. Everything is. Plug her in. For the love of. Sarina, Sarina, Sarina, Sarina.

1:43 A.M.

Sam Mongoose, owner of the city's #1 jazz club, surveys The Cat's Pajamas. With him as always is Rico, the Max Cubanista of Mongoose's. The real Max Cubanista pumps and mugs onstage. Seeing these men cross the bar like a storm cloud, Max dons an unnatural smile, leans over to Gus, and purrs: "What is this phenomenal bullshit?"

1:45 A.M.

*T*he band goes on break.

Lookie loo and how do you do, Principal Randles is on a roll. She sits at a back table at The Cat's Pajamas, one shoulder thrust out of her one-shouldered dress toward heaven, with the tax attorney, who has a pointed Main Line nose and hulking arms. Arms that make a girl feel slender. This man has been chortling at her school stories all night—and she always thought they were boring! He would be happy to do her taxes, he said. *My taxes?* she had breathed, allowing her inflection to reach its most sultry hilt so that he'd get that she was not talking about taxes. Yes, he said, so no-nonsense, so pointy-nosey, submitting them early is money in your pocket. Take that, glue-covered, poop-tongued children! Take that, female pattern baldness! She angles her neck to reveal more of what was once described as ivory skin. By her grandmother, to the family doctor. She says, "When the band comes back, let's dance!" "What?" he says and she insists, "dance!" "Did you say something, it's so loud in here!" "Dance!" she says. "Dance!"

The tax attorney panics. "Dance?"

1:45 A.M.

*T*he band goes on break.

Sarina and her ex-husband stand outside on the curb, sucking on Parliament Lights.

"What is it?" Marcos says. "You love him? You don't care that he's married?"

"They're separated," she says.

"Well." He takes a drag. "Shit."

"I like spending time with him." She kicks at the building's bricks.

"Nothing clarifies feelings faster than jealousy."

"You and Cassidy serious?"

He shakes his head. "As serious as you can be with a girl who has never heard of Steely Dan."

"You're kidding."

"She thought it was a dish cleaner."

Ben and Cassidy appear in the doorway.

"Who wants a drink?" Cassidy says.

"I do, darling." Marcos toes out his cigarette.

"I'll fix you one." Her volume startles a trio of texting girls. "Am I talking to you?" she says, before disappearing inside with Marcos.

Sarina should be happy to be back in what has become their ready position of the night; however, Ben seems like a different person, one who has danced capably with someone else. Twenty

256

years have passed since the night of their prom yet he is the same. His ludicrous way of smiling all the time. The cheap green of his eyes, not the color of shamrocks (something lucky) or emeralds (something valuable), but of dying field grass, chestnut wheat. The figure of his pupil moves like a horse amid these lousy, dry grains. Are they hazel or brown? DECIDE. His untried lawyer's hands. Unable to build a bureau. The cavity of his morals: leaving her over and over, for this theater girl or that wife. Flat-footed on the pavement. His eyebrows assist in all of his famous expressions, the one where he hopes the magic trick will please the little girl: magic tricks for kids, the preoccupations of a never-do-well, never do for her, never a groomsman, always a groom. Look at him, one hand pocketed, the other flirting around the base of his sand-colored hair. Look at him: the rose color creeping into his cheeks— the first signal he is about to laugh. Look at him. She looks at him.

"Would you like another drink, Miss Greene?"
She nods.
"Let me guess. Whiskey?"
He pauses, framed in the doorway. She sees how he will be as an old man. Finely shaped calves in gray pants. The sallow, lightable cheeks. This is the meanest thing he can do: know her drink and act tenderly. To show her the exact form of what she can sit beside but not

257

keep. In the jaundiced light of a streetlamp, Sarina realizes why people have children: to see the face of the one they love at the ages they've missed, to see his eyes on a son she could teach to use scissors.

1:46 A.M.

*T*he guitar case is already laid out on the table in the back room. Lorca unzips it and reveals the golden body of his father's 1932 D'Angelico Snakehead. Its tanned back and S nostrils are graceful on the ugly table, making everything else in the room seem shopworn.

Mongoose caresses the guitar's smooth face. Veins on his nose and cheeks map out the course of his drinking. "You've kept her in great shape."

Sonny, Max, Gus, and Alex enter the room, significantly increasing the sequin ratio. Max strikes what he thinks is a threatening stance. "Why is Francis's guitar out?"

"Why aren't you onstage?" Lorca says.

"We're on break, buddy."

Mongoose picks up the guitar. Nausea runs through Lorca. Except for cleanings, the Snakehead hasn't left its wall case for fifty years. The guitar belongs to the club, sanctifying its sinners, but if he loses the club, she'll be slumped against the wall of his apartment, sanctifying the roaches.

"You guys sound good tonight," Rico says. "But I'd play the fourth finger on that B flat."

"You know where you can put your fourth finger?" says Max.

"Up my ass?" Rico says.

Max says, "Up mine, buddy."

"Would you like that?"

The room smells like deli meat. Sonny's bald spot flushes. Flecks of perspiration dot the sides of his mouth. Lorca tells him to sit down but instead he stands behind him breathing thickly onto his neck, a presence Lorca realizes he appreciates. Mongoose plays a chord on the Snakehead, the first sound Lorca has heard her make in years. It's not possible for her to be in tune after these years, yet she is. Mongoose passes the guitar to Rico, who fondles her strings.

"You'd think you would save this for him," Mongoose says, meaning Alex.

Alex's lip curls like he might spit. "Screw off, old man."

"I see the family resemblance." Mongoose laughs. "I'll take it." He acts as if buying one of the greatest guitars ever built for thousands less than it's worth is a favor. He pulls an envelope from his pocket and hands it to Lorca. "It's a shame, is all."

Rico fidgets: velvet lapel, a continent of dirt on his neck, thick calluses on the pads of his fingers. "First Louisa, now your guitar."

Sonny advances. "What'd you say?"

"I said, first the girl, now the guitar."

Max's eyes are slick with excitement. "Are we getting in a fight?"

"We're not getting in a fight," Lorca says.

Alex stands in the semicircle around the body of the Snakehead. In the overhead lamp, his black hair shines blue.

"What's up, kid?" Rico says.

Alex brings his fist into Rico's jaw clean like a poem. Rico flops and spits.

Lorca steadies the guitar on the swiveling table.

Rico's trajectory pins Sonny against the wall. Alex's body is arched in the follow-through of his punch. Whatever follows will hinge on what Rico does when he gets to his feet. Trepidation stubbles the air. Alex doesn't wait. Head bobbing to some unheard music, he hits Rico again. Sonny's mouth falls open. No one wants to fight, but now the kid has made a promise. The table swivels again as Rico slings all of his weight against Alex. Their fall launches a folding chair across the floor. Mongoose tries to stop them and inadvertently elbows Sonny. They lose their footing. The room becomes a wash of sequins and polyester.

"Jesus," Lorca says. "We're a hundred years old!"

The swinging lamp throws half-moons onto the fray. No man in the room is a fighter. They are barely men. Their jabs and dives are put-ons, versions of things they've seen in movies. Alex is the only one with aptitude.

"Alex," Lorca yells. "Watch your hands." Max leaps onto the table, pumping his fists and yawping. He overturns a napkin holder onto the scramble of flesh below him. Mongoose and Sonny skitter on the floor and careen into Lorca, who has time to say "Shit" before his ankle relents, sending them hurtling in an unholy wreck toward the table. The force of their impact jackknifes the table's legs. For a moment everything in the room halts, as if even the table is unwilling to eject Max and the Snakehead. Lorca reaches pointlessly toward the guitar. The Snakehead vaults, hits ground, and slides toward the wall ("Vanilla," Louisa said when he bought her that first milkshake at the Red Lion Diner, pronouncing it with the telltale "ella" that marked her as a city girl, the beveled glass reflecting the arcade, reflecting the bumpers in the parking lot, reflecting new love's bald pate) before being skewered by the table, several chairs, Max, a handful of outdated napkins, and two middle-aged men fumbling for the punch line of a joke that has gone too far.

A dull pop. A sudden, broken bone. Lorca's nostrils fill with the dust of an ashtray. He shakes and shakes. Lorca thinks Sonny is helping him up, but he is clearing him from the collapse, yelling at everyone to move away from the guitar. Sonny swivels to face the panting men.

The fracture goes clean down her body. Her neck is snapped off but dangles by the loyal and steadfast E. The room is emergency quiet. The fight is abandoned. Lorca delivers the two pieces of his father's guitar into the snakeskin case. He kneels and throws up into the trash can by his desk.

The room clears. The Cubanistas go back to the stage. Lorca can hear them launch into a floor-stomper from where he crouches over the can. The room is empty except for Mongoose, holding out a napkin. Lorca uses it to clean his mouth. He will take a stool at the bar and drink until he has erased himself.

Mongoose tucks the envelope of money into his jacket. "I want to say something to you," he says. "I had nothing to do with Charlie." Lorca attempts to speak, but Mongoose interrupts him. "You guys forget. He was like my brother. All these years not talking for what?" Mongoose says. "I miss you guys."

It is not the first time Mongoose has denied involvement with Charlie's death, but it is the first time Lorca considers it. He nods. Throwing up has made his head feel better than it has all day. "I need a favor," he says. "For my son."

The two men stare at the broken guitar.

Mongoose says, "Seems like the least I can do."

1:58 A.M.

Still hidden in the coats, Madeleine and her still-flippering heart.

The band returns from break. The young guitarist taps his boot on the lowest rung of his stool and repositions the guitar on his knee. The piano player pulls from his bottle. They start a song that is so familiar to Madeleine that at first she doesn't recognize it. When she does, it becomes impossible for her to hide in the back. She knows the song and she wants everyone to know she knows the song.

She elbows through the coats and opens her mouth to sing.

No sound comes. Her throat refuses clear passage. She advances into the crowd and stamps her foot to get it going. "Hey!" she pleads. "Come on!" The crowd turns away from the musicians onstage, surprised to find a new show behind them. One face turns and is immediately delighted. It is Ben, holding a beer in one hand, a drink, his wallet, and a pack of cigarettes in another. Miss Greene is there, too. Her eyes grow as wide as the Schuylkill River, and as muddy, and as hard to pass. But Madeleine is finished with rules. This struggle is between her and her nerves. She batters at herself but her voice will not come.

"Make room," Ben says.

Madeleine pulses. The first verse has passed; the first chorus is halfway over. Still, she cannot produce a sound. One hand hipped, the other keeping time like she has practiced only instead of on the hard floor of her bedroom, her child size nines are rooted on the hard floor of the city's #2 jazz club.

So Madeleine has followed them here, to sing on this stage. The morning in church, the apple, the lice, collect in Sarina's mind as she hatches this wild girl battle herself. She decides that one person will get what they want tonight. She takes Madeleine's hand, leads her to the front, and halts, perhaps waiting for a rational objection to intercede. When none does, she lifts Madeleine onto the stage in front of a microphone the little girl instinctively lowers to account for her humble stature.

"Madeleine," Miss Greene says. "Sing."

1:59 A.M.

Madeleine opens her mouth to sing.

1:59 A.M.

Principal Randles struggles to batten down the flummoxing corners of her mind. It is not possible the Altimari girl is onstage, opening her mouth to sing.

1:59 A.M.

Madeleine smells the figgy odor of perspiring musicians. Anxiety whisks her vision. The moment seems to be skipping like one of her father's records. She opens her mouth to sing.

Her voice doesn't show.

2:00 A.M.

Who is this scrappy tomato? The band members communicate without words. They know what to do when a singer chokes. They vamp. If this little girl wants to start something, they'll support it, but if not, they'll bolt. There's a difference between people who can sing in their showers and people who can sing onstage.

Max grins at the little girl. "Shit or get off the pot," he says.

Still vamping. Still nothing from the little girl.

He nods to Gus lift off into another song. But then the little girl insists into the microphone:

Baby, here I am, by the railroad track!

Max motions for the others to stay on the same tip. The tomato is going to try it.

Madeleine is singing!

The caramel apples do not concern her. Her roachy apartment does not concern her. The young guitarist does not concern her, though she senses he is moving his music over and under her singing. The thorny issues of her particular life do not concern her. Even her mother. The only thought Madeleine has is, when she is singing,

singing. There is only the way the song feels in her throat.

Waiting for my baby!

In a white room lit by a white candle, Madeleine is the white candle. Madeleine is the white room. Born perfect from her perfect mother and fucked up by her fucked-up father, one holy, catholic, and apostolic song. It is the rest of her life rising to meet her like heat from the sidewalk and she knows it like she knows to take the A train when you want to find yourself in Harlem.

He's comin' back!

She sparkles, she goddamns, when it's time for the highest note, she gathers the reins of her diaphragm and soars. Even the musicians doff their impassive expressions. The song is over and everything around Madeleine gets loud with applause, yet somehow she hears the young guitarist say, "What's next, little girl?"

Madeleine calls out the song like she's done it countless times, like she and he have a routine they've hammered out in late-night venues. Madeleine calls out "Blossom's Blues," then immediately regrets it. No one knows Blossom Dearie except her dead mother who would make her dead too if she caught her here, but

Madeleine's self-lecture is interrupted by the first chords of "Blossom's Blues" and if she keeps berating herself she will miss her—

My name is Blossom, I was raised in a lion's den.
My nightly occupation is stealing other women's men.

It is Christmas Eve Eve and Madeleine is singing on a stage and you can shove your caramel apple up your ass, Clare Kelly.

2:00 A.M.

ou hear the one about the talking dog?" Lorca says. He and Mongoose are in the hallway, walking back to the bar. "A man and a dog walk into a club. The man says to the club owner, 'This here is a talking dog. We've just come from Europe where we killed every night, so you have to give us a gig.' The club owner says sure, but he'll have to test the dog. 'You've just come from Europe,' he says to the dog. 'How was your trip?' The dog says, 'Ruff!' The club owner nods. 'How was the flight?' he says. The dog says, 'Ruff!' The club owner thinks a minute. 'What were the headlines of today's paper?' he says. The dog stays silent. 'See here,' the club owner says, 'tell me what the headlines were on today's paper.' No dice. The dog doesn't answer. The club owner kicks them out. They go home and the man is furious. He screams at the dog, 'Why did you not tell the man what the headlines were on today's paper?' And the dog says, 'You know damn well I can't read.'"

Mongoose snorts, nods. Then he lifts his chin, listening. "Who's that singing, Lorca?"

They muscle through the standing crowd. Onstage a young girl (eleven? twelve?) is singing.

"Christ," Mongoose says. "Child labor." Then, impressed, "She's tearing it up."

This girl isn't tall enough to see over the audience. Alex jags in and out of her runs. He stomps his foot and guffaws toward Gus. He seems to be unable to stop smiling. Something about the facility of his wrists flexing over the fretboard. Something about his upturned face. Lorca sees his son the way a stranger would who happened in from the street, and realizes there can be no life for his son other than the one music will make for him.

"We have to stop them." Sonny's eyes are panicked. "It's two A.M. Christ, Lorca. Wake up."

Sonny is right, but Lorca doesn't intervene or even move toward the stage. He listens to his son play, and a feeling settles over him that is at once so whole, so undeniably itself, it has to be joy.

2:00 A.M.

*B*en places his lips against Sarina's. She raises her chin to make it easier for him. It's more of a press than a kiss. A place marker.

The feeling at the base of Sarina's stomach is akin to the promise of snow. Ben releases her but does not move away. Sarina touches her bottom lip for reference.

Madeleine is singing.

Principal Randles sits in a booth by the window, her will climbing and falling against the cage of her decorum. Something about this girl and her song is so rapturous, so influential, that even the tax attorney begins to move the lower half of his body. She will not cause a scene. She will not rise up from where she sits. It will not be the Winter Assembly again. But then the girl hits one pure note that shimmers into vibrato and the principal's dominion over her actions slips. She's standing, but she will not leer over the table. Fine, it is permittable to leer if only his attention stays on the stage. But the tax attorney, twitching with rhythm, feels her movement behind him. How can she explain? How can she battle the urge to hold him? She will say a cheerful remark and sit back down. She cannot think of a cheerful remark. The girl alights into an array of short notes, each one hammering a rib in the principal's rib cage. The tax attorney's cheeks are the color of sheets she can't afford. Three thousand thread count. She clutches at them. She will not put her tongue on him. She will not put her tongue on him again. He tries to shake her grip with a stilted laugh.

She will let him go. After this lick. After the next. But his skin tastes like olives and she loves olives. She takes unhurried, indulgent licks.

It is the Winter Assembly again, only this time instead of mauling Kevin, the unfairly muscled janitor, she mauls the tax attorney, who under "Special Interests" on his profile wrote, *Your wok or mine?*

Release him, she begs herself. He is openly struggling. But her ancestors were electricians and plumbers. She can devastate chestnuts in her grip. She moans into his ear. The tax attorney bats at the ground with his feet. People at other tables gape. She cannot stop, dear God let me stop, she cannot stop. She drags her tongue from the base of his chin to the corners of his petrified eyes.

2:01 A.M.

*T*he world is fair tonight, so fair that Madeleine is filled to her ears with fairness; it is fair, fair, fair. She prances back and forth on the stage, delivering this line to that person, and that line to this. The audience looks delighted except for this man who has pounded onto the stage and is cuffing her forearm past the point of fairness.

Madeleine recoils.

"Attention everyone," the man says. No one listens. The man "Attentions" again.

His gruff words do not match the gentle disposition of the audience. The guitarist stops playing and the drummer stills. The cheering subsides.

It is Len Thomas, flanked by plainclothes officers.

"What time is it?" Lorca says. A cursory survey of the club tells him it is over capacity by roughly seventy-five people. A musician onstage is smoking. He is smoking. It is past two A.M. A minor is singing. In addition to the fine he already owes, who can imagine what kind of improbable debt is being calculated on the notepad of Len Thomas.

"This club is being closed by order of the city. Everyone is expected to leave immediately except those I will keep for questioning."

Madeleine shakes the man off. She has nowhere to go but into the bank of people who part as she jumps. They clog her running path. She counters, jockeys, double jockeys. *Who are you who is that who was that?* Toward the tonsil of pale night that peeks into the club at every entrance or exit through its heavy doors, Madeleine runs and Madeleine runs.

Miss Greene and Ben catch her at the door.

"I sang," Madeleine says, but that doesn't get to it as deeply as she feels so she says it again, harder.

The door is blocked by an officer. "She'll need to speak to us. Are you her mother?"

"I'm her teacher," Sarina says.

"You can stay." He points to Ben. "Is this your husband?"

"Friend," Sarina says.

"He'll have to go."

"I'll wait outside," Ben says.

"No one will be allowed to wait outside," the officer assures him.

He opens the door and lets people go one by one. The crowd steals glances at Madeleine as they heave toward the door. Ben takes Sarina's hand to steel them against the current.

"Wait," he says. "This can't be the end."

Sarina searches his eyes as if in them she has misplaced a set of keys.

Madeleine wants to tell them to hurry it up but

her teacher's pained smile stops her. It is the one she uses when a student struggles for an answer, to tell them she believes they have it in them. Even Madeleine knows to stay silent. If you are anything other than humbled in the presence of love, you are not in the presence of love.

"Keep me updated on the status of your everything," Sarina says, and releases Ben's hand. The space between them fills with other people.

2:30 A.M.

A serious-faced boy approaches the bar, where Madeleine and Miss Greene wait to be interviewed. "Do you remember me?"

Madeleine nods. "You're the guitarist."

"I'm also the son of the guy whose club you helped close."

Madeleine shifts her weight to her right, leading foot. She will spring through the club and out the quilted door if shit goes down.

"Girl." He reaches out an arm to pin her. "No one's mad."

"Your dad is."

"He's always mad." The boy grins. "How did you end up here?"

"I snuck here," Madeleine says, "because I wanted to sing."

His eyes register recognition but when he speaks, his tone is unfriendly. "Why?"

Madeleine is too tired to be tough. "Because they never let me sing at church," she says. "Or at assemblies. Or anywhere. It's always Clare Kelly. They say she's the best singer in school, but her phrasing and pitch are bullshit."

"Madeleine," Miss Greene warns.

The boy works something over in his jaw. "You should worry less about whoever-the-hell and more about the fact that you can't pace yourself. You almost blew it in the first verse."

Madeleine knows he's right. "Will you teach me?" she says. "I can sing while you play."

"How old are you?" he says.

"Fourteen."

He spits on the ground.

She is unaccustomed to wanting someone's approval and can't shear the desperation from her voice. "Nine," she says. "But my birthday's in two days."

"I don't play with children," he says.

One of the officers emerges from the back and calls her name. "Screw off then."

In the back room, an officer named Len Thomas assures her that there will only be a few questions. A man she does not recognize takes the chair next to her. "I have some questions, too."

"Mr. Vega, this is not appropriate."

"Call me Sonny." He winks at Madeleine. "I won't make a peep."

"Name?" Officer Thomas begins. "Address and age?"

"Who do we know?" Sonny says. "Who's your family?"

"My father is Mark Altimari," Madeline says. "He used to be a vendor on Ninth Street."

"That's not it." Sonny frowns.

"Mr. Vega," Officer Thomas warns.

"Madeleine Altimari," she tells him. "Eighteen

278

South Ninth Street. Aged nine years and three hundred sixty-three days."

"How did you come to find yourself here tonight?"

"It's a long story," she says.

Officer Thomas's eyebrows jolt toward the ceiling. "I've got time."

"I climbed out my window and walked."

"You walked from Ninth?"

"It's not that far if you take South all the way," Sonny says. "Who's your singing teacher?"

Madeleine turns to face him. "I don't have one."

"You sing like that with no teacher?"

"My mother taught me."

Underneath Officer Thomas's collar, a flush of red. "Mr. Vega, in many courts of law what you are doing would be considered interfering with police procedure." He turns back to Madeleine. "What you're saying is that tonight you climbed out of your window and walked across the city, to this club, got onstage, and sang of your own volition?"

"I wanted to sing," Madeleine says. She is not afraid of police officers. Her only fear is roaches. At home on a recipe card labeled MISCELLANY, under NEVER SHOW UP TO SOMEONE'S HOME EMPTY-HANDED and DON'T TRUST A GIRL WITH NO GIRLFRIENDS, were the words: DON'T TRUST COPS.

The cop looks baffled, but the man named Sonny seems satisfied. "Your mother must be a great singer," he says.

"My mother is dead," Madeleine says. "Rose Santiago takes care of me."

Sonny leans back in his chair, beaming. "Bingo."

Officer Thomas makes furious scratches onto his pad.

Madeleine waits for Miss Greene to be interviewed at the front of the bar, where young people smoke and curse. She finds a cigarette in the front pocket of her vest. The young guitarist strikes a match and lights it for her.

"All right," he says. "I'll teach you."

She chokes on an inhalation of smoke. "I don't have any money."

"I don't care about money."

She offers her hand and they shake.

"What's it like to be born on Christmas?" he says.

She thinks about it. "It sucks."

Sarina and Madeleine walk to Market Street to find a cab. A car slows next to them; its passenger-side window descends and through it Principal Randles calls their names. "I'll drive you home." Her tone is official, as if she is announcing the results of CYO games over the PA.

"No, thank you," Madeleine says.

"I can't have you walking by yourself," the principal says.

"We would love a ride." Sarina climbs into the front seat and gives directions. The principal turns the heat higher and adjusts the vents so they point to Madeleine, who climbs into the back.

"Seat belt," the principal reminds her.

The girl sighs and clicks her belt into place.

Sarina eyes her boss, who wears lipstick the color of cotton candy. "How lucky you happened to be driving by." A satiny dress peeks through the opening of her coat. Are those pearl earrings? The principal does not seem willing to explain. Sarina is not willing to explain either, so they are even.

They drive in silence. Crisp lawns, an over-turned plastic Santa.

"Is that 'Wonderwall'?" Principal Randles says.

Sarina's phone is ringing in the bowels of her bag. She doesn't recognize the number and dumps the call into voice mail.

Madeleine sulks in the unlit swell of the backseat. "Why do you hate me so much?"

"Madeleine," Sarina says. "That's not polite."

They stop at a red light. In a store window, a sign promises furniture sales in the new year. Principal Randles clicks on her turn signal. She clears her throat. "It was hard to be young with your mom."

The light changes to green. They have almost reached their apartment complex.

Madeleine can feel the principal staring at her in the rearview mirror but refuses to acknowledge her. She is no longer a student at Saint Anthony's.

"Your mother," the principal says, "used to shrug whenever someone else would. Even on television. If someone on television shrugged, she shrugged."

"I didn't know that." Madeleine's eyes widen. "I do that, too."

Principal Randles taps the steering wheel. "There you go."

"Count to seven," Sarina says. "Then stop because we're here."

"Merry Christmas." The principal brakes. "See you after the holiday."

"Madeleine is expelled," Sarina reminds her.

The principal activates the emergency brake. Her voice is punctured. "Come in after the holiday," she says. "I'll unexpel you." She swerves trimly into the street and drives away. Sarina and Madeleine watch her, breath pillowing in front of them.

"I guess that's a happy ending," Sarina says.

"I guess."

Sarina pauses at her door. "Good night, Madeleine. I expect I'll have to tell Mrs. Santiago about this in the morning."

"Good night, Miss Greene. I expect she'll blow her fucking lid."

Madeleine climbs into her window. She counts thirty beats, then runs the stairs to the roof. The cars on the Second Street Bridge launch over the river, blowing their staccato horns. The rush of the El, a swelling of cymbals. The big sky over the stadium is lit by morning stars. The shivering hump on the wire becomes a glissando of crows that fly toward the statue of Saint Anthony. There they part into three flapping factions: one takes the alleys on Ninth, one heads toward the river, one goes west to hop the El. Who can be certain which way is faster? You can't say you know a city unless you know three ways to everywhere.

Madeleine swings her legs over the edge of the roof. *I sang on a stage.* She is close enough to high-five Saint Anthony but doesn't because no matter what kind of thrilling night you've had, you do not bother saints this way.

3:15 A.M.

Sarina, it's Georgie. You're probably sleeping. I couldn't sleep. I wanted to say . . . Pepper, get down! I'm happy you came over tonight. And. I realize you've had a rough time but . . . you seem great. I'd like to go to that crochet class you mentioned. We could have dinner. Stop eating that, Pepper. I won't be good at it, but I'd like to go. The last thing I made was a birdhouse and the hole was so small birds couldn't fit. They'd stick their beaks in and try to wiggle through but they couldn't. It broke my heart. Not even those tiny birds. The ones that hop all over the sand at the shore. What are they called? Sparrows!

4:00 A.M.

Age?" Len's pen is poised over his notebook.
Alex chews gum, his expression blank.
"Twenty-one."

"Come on," Len sighs, looking at Lorca.

"Twenty-one," Lorca says.

Len lets Alex go and he and Aruna Sha sit cross-legged on the club's floor surrounded by their attending pack of jawing teenagers. Alex preens amid their compliments. The Main Line kid yammers about a show at Ortlieb's when John Coltrane literally set the house on fire. He uses a tone that implies Alex will never be as good as Coltrane, to temper the effect Alex is having on their friends. Lorca has been around guys like him for years. The jawing gives him away. It's the mark of someone who can't play. No one with chops yaps about it. They're humble because they're in service. They know they have to practice when they are filled with love. When they are filled with bile. When the sun is out and everyone with a palpably alive soul is on the beach, they are in wood-paneled dumps, practicing. Until they ruin any chance at being substantial and there is no soul on earth who will have them.

Through that, you practice. What hurts most, you do again. Away from the living people you

285

practice for. Toward the shaking, fleeting thing you only let yourself half-believe in. Most times you do not find it but in search of it, you practice, scared of your ability to be so wholly alone. You don't have time to boast or judge.

If this is the life his son wants, Lorca can at least help him as much as he can. He stands above the group and addresses the Main Line kid. "Literally?" he says. "Burned the house down?"

The kid's smirk recedes. "Not literally."

"You were good tonight," Lorca says to his son.

"I showboated Emo's solo."

The kid pipes up, but Lorca interrupts. "You didn't showboat."

"Well, I did."

"I'd tell you," Lorca says, "if you did."

"Can I play here again then?"

Len calls another witness to the back room. "Probably not here," Lorca says.

"Jazz is a dying art form anyway." The Main Line kid makes this statement to the screen of his phone as his thumb jabs the keyboard.

Lorca ignores him. "Mongoose is going to take you. It'll be weekends to start. Friday and Saturday nights and Sunday brunch. Rehearsals once a week. You won't have time to hang out with . . ." He looks at the kid. "You won't have time for much else besides school. If this is okay with you, I'll tell Mongoose."

"It's okay with me," Alex says.

"You were good tonight," Lorca says. "But you have to get healthy."

Alex beams. He tells his father he will.

Lorca turns to the Main Line kid. "John Coltrane never played Ortlieb's. He was dead for a million years by the time that joint opened. He did play here, though. Plenty of times."

The kid's face falls off a cliff.

Len is finished with his interviews. It is time for the club to clear out.

"Get what's important to you," Lorca says.

The boys shoulder their guitars, Max grabs his hair grease, Gus carries the model airplane, finished except for the racing stripes. They smoke outside while Lorca and Len finish up in the bar. Lorca turns off the overhead lamp and closes the door to the back. He still wears the T-shirt and jeans from the day before when all he had to worry about was replacing a drum set.

"It hasn't even been a day." Len rips a new citation from his pad. He seems in awe of Lorca's inability to keep himself straight for twenty-four hours. "I was just here this morning. Did I not make it clear?"

"You did everything you could," Lorca says, locking the back room. He kills the lights in the hallways and bathrooms, the wall lights, the bar lights. He lowers the heat. The floor will have to stay a mess until whatever day he is allowed ck in. He hoists the broken Snakehead over his noulder, wincing at its upsetting, multiple ounds, and joins the others outside.

"The Daphne girl has moved on." From Max to Gus. Sonny points to where the girl in yellow heels is huddled over the model plane with Gus —Gus explaining something as she nods, intently.

"That's what they call a safe bet," Lorca says.

Len and the officers nail the doors shut. The last of the witnesses turn back when they hear the splitting wood echo against the corroded windows on the street. Len hammers a nail into the door while clenching the next one in his teeth. Lorca stands to the side. He has time to consider what is happening, to repent or beg or search for loopholes. But instead he thinks about the way Louisa says the word *experiment*. Ex-spear-iment. He watches his son whisper into Aruna's ear. In the darkness, the river gasps.

CLOSED DUE TO VIOLATION OF CITY LAW.

Len pockets the hammer and motions for the officers to leave. "Take care, Mr. Lorca." He walks toward his car and pauses. "I'm sorry you lost your club." The back of his collar is still not fully folded over his tie. Lorca wants to reach out and fix it. Len checks his seat belt twice before pulling out and swerving around Gray Gus, who is reasoning with the airplane's finicky remote control. The blue switches and red knobs that should convince the plane into the air fail to get a response. Gus raps on it.

Lorca says, "Alex knew exactly where Max was going in every song."

Sonny coughs, refolds the sleeves of his trench coat. "The kid is good."

"You have to rehearse to get that good," Lorca says. "You wouldn't know anything about that, would you?"

Sonny blinks. "I would not."

"Maybe it's time for a vacation. Throw our rods in the car and drive down the coast." Lorca calls to Alex. "You want to go fishing?"

"Sure," Alex says.

Sonny frowns. "Whose car?"

The plane is alive. It taxis down Front Street to the end of the building where it dies with no ceremony. Gus fiddles with the control pad.

"That's too bad," Daphne says. A rhinestone winks on each of her painted nails.

They decide to go to the Red Lion Diner. "We'll walk up Girard," Max says.

"The alleys are faster," Sonny insists.

"Your ass the alleys are faster," Max snorts. "You want to get there today?"

The party walks ahead, leaving Gus and Daphne alone with the grounded plane. Gus tries switches, hoping for a new development. Teetering on her heels, Daphne lists what she will order when they get to the diner.

"The biggest omelet they have," she says. "Mushrooms and cheese and sausage and broccoli . . ."

"And gravy?"

"Gravy and biscuits and a waffle. They're going to need two men to bring it to the table. And a *basket* of fries."

"A suitcase of fries, darlin'," Gus says.

"A wheelbarrow."

"It's a shame," Cassidy says. "My first day was my last day. Did you hear that little girl? How do you learn how to sing like that?"

Max pauses in his argument with Sonny. "You don't, angel. You get born like that."

Behind them, where he walks with his son, Lorca realizes there will be no club to open in the morning. A relief he did not anticipate unrolls in his chest. "I'm going to be around more now," Lorca says.

"All right," Alex says.

"So, how's school?"

"Not good."

Celebration behind them. Gus has found the right combination of switches and buttons and the plane has roared to life again. It races toward them and tries a leap but cannot achieve the sky. It takes a jagged, desperate run.

Sonny squints. "Bring her nose up!"

Gus glares at the control. "I know, bring her nose up."

290

"Get her up, old man," yells Sonny. Then he mutters to Lorca, "He has to get the nose up or it won't fly."

Daphne believes in the plane. When everyone else is certain it won't succeed, when the other girls turn toward the direction of ham and coffee, she raises her arms in a V. "Go, plane, go!"

The plane opts for different tacks but none of them gets it airborne. Its skin shakes with effort. Just when it seems like it has given up, it performs a successful hop into the air. It feathers higher, clearing the group. They wheel around to watch it ascend.

"You're still going, though," Lorca says. "To school?"

Alex grins. "Still going."

"That's a start," Lorca says.

The plane gulps, goes higher. It shakes off its panic. The body stills, the buzz settles into itself and becomes a hum. Gus's face reddens. Daphne jumps in her heels, cheering. Everyone is cheering.

Lorca whistles. "Look at that."

He and his son watch the plane in the sky.

4:20 A.M.

Ben dozes on the Market-Frankford El platform, head tucked into his coat. Below, in the parking lot of a discount food store, a streetlight shines on one lone car.

He'll sleep here until the first train of the new day erupts into the station. Once seated, he will rewind the evening and begin playback with the moment he, shaking himself out of his coat, saw Sarina Greene. No, beginning with the afternoon phone call when the name Sarina Greene uprooted him. No, beginning way before that, with yellow chiffon and his brother's majestic Mustang.

In her kitchen, Sarina adds cherries to a bowl of vanilla ice cream. She wants to finish *Sunshine the Dragon* before she falls asleep. She is almost at the end.

It is cold on the platform but not unbearable. Everyone in the city is dreaming, their refrigerators stacked with holiday platters covered in aluminum foil. It is Christmas Eve, Ben realizes. Tomorrow he and his parents will eat Chinese food and watch television in their slippers. His brother will call and he will tell him he spent the night walking the city with Sarina Greene.

The station clerk appears on the platform and lights a cigarette. "Shouldn't be long," he says, about the train.

Ben nods, nestles farther into the coat.

"Look." The clerk points.

With only a few pages left, a stray thought pulls Sarina out of the book.

Many years before, at a party for something she cannot remember, she and her father are sent to the store for candles. Her father hoists her into his arms and carries her away from the celebration. The bristle of his cheek. The keys rattling in his free hand. Balloons on the mailbox. Sarina feels lucky to have a father who can carry her with one hand. At the doorway, they frown. The day has turned stony and cold. Sarina does not have her coat, but getting it would send her back into the house, sifting through aunts and kids' toys and junk. Her father says she doesn't need it.

"But, Dad," she presses. "What if it rains?"

Even as a little girl, such a worrier.

"If it rains," he says, "we'll get wet."

In the lot below the El platform, a shopping cart rolls down an incline toward the parked hatchback. The cart's progress is slow but unhindered. It is gaining speed.

The clerk exhales smoke into a cloud the shape of a horse. "That cart's going to hit that car," he says.

293

Ben watches (Sarina closes the book) and can hear the ambition of the cart's wheels carry it down the broad swath of asphalt. (Sarina turns off the lamp.) "No," he says. "Everything is going to be fine."

6:30 A.M.

Madeleine knows the jig is up. Miss Greene will be coming by to rat her out, so as Mrs. Santiago uncovers the coffee machine and fires the burners, Madeleine comes clean. She explains the apples, the expulsion, the lice. She orbits Mrs. Santiago, a chattering binary star, while the woman shovels pastries from box to case. Miss Greene, the guitarist, the unexpulsion. She skips the part about the stolen apple. Pedro circles her circling Mrs. Santiago. The three-partied planetary system moves to the table where Madeleine, emptied, waits for her punishment.

Mrs. Santiago stirs her espresso, deep in thought. Finally she speaks. "This"—she points to Madeleine, then to herself—"is not going to work unless you are honest with me. Do you understand?"

"I do," says Madeleine.

"I don't think you do. I will not be able to handle you not being honest with me. That will break me."

Madeleine squirms in her seat. "I stole an apple."

"Is that all of it?"

"Yes," Madeleine says.

"Is it?"

"I promise."

"I believe you." Mrs. Santiago nods. "Now you must sing for me. Sing," she says. "Now."

Madeleine stands. She places a steadying hand against one of the display cases and the other on her hip.

I hear music, mighty fine music

Neither the previous night's excitement nor the fact that she hasn't eaten breakfast shows up in her voice. It is stronger than it was onstage. She trills. She thinks about pacing.

Mrs. Santiago's head plumps, sheathed in sweat.

Madeleine quiets. "Do you need water?"

"Sing!"

Madeleine builds to the big finish. She lets the note warble for an extra few measures.

Mrs. Santiago bravos out of her chair and pulls Madeleine into a hug. Her apron smells like warm chicken and cranberry candle. She releases Madeleine and grasps the counter. Her feet leave her shoes and hover several inches off the ground. She returns to them. Her ears turn the color of autumn leaves. She jolts upward again, this time with her shoes. Madeleine can see her own frightened face in the woman's watering eyes.

"I feel strange." Mrs. Santiago throws open the front door and staggers outside. Madeleine follows. The woman takes a few steps and ascends, as if climbing an invisible staircase. She turns her bulbous head—it is shiny like the counters of the Red Lion Diner—and her features are at sea on it. Her small mouth has become the balloon's cinched knot. One of her apron strings breaks with a sharp *thwack!*

"Mrs. Santiago!" Madeleine snatches at the woman's skirt.

"For Pete's sake, you're almost ten, call me Rose." She rises over the carousel horse. She attempts to bank but cannot steer down. *Thwack!* The other apron string. A gust of wind takes her higher. She has almost reached roof level.

"Come down. Rose!"

"I can see everyone's laundry!" Mrs. Santiago cries. "All of their shirts and pants, hanging. What a funny thing."

"Are you in pain?" Madeleine says.

The force of the woman's giggling carries her sideways and surprises a wire of wrens. She grows serious. "Start the coffee. Make sure the sausage doesn't burn. Wipe the cases. When I come back, I want to be able to see my face in them." She wags her arms toward the loitering stars. Under her, Pedro barks and makes erratic circles. "Oh, hush. I'll be back in a while." One clog loses its grip on her foot. It claps against a neighbor's patio. "I can see everyone's holiday lights! I can see the ships at the dock!"

She drifts farther away from Madeleine and the

dog who, stunned by her rebuke, calms. Her other clog falls and clatters against some unseen hard thing. It's a landmark morning, she tells the stray cat hiding in a bank of chopped evergreens.

Madeleine watches until Mrs. Santiago is hundreds of rooftops away, then she and Pedro go inside. She extinguishes the burner under the sausage and starts the coffee. Pedro circles into a resting position on the floor and falls asleep. Madeleine retrieves her notebook from her backpack and borrows the baking timer.

She starts the shimmy. Shoulders, shoulders, shoulders.

The timer beeps. Madeleine marks down *thirty seconds*. The shimmying was spirited and even. Not bad, she decides, and allows herself a B plus.

Don't get cocky, Madeleine. It's been a good night but you are still a poor, motherless girl in old stockings.

The room fills with the smell of coffee. The pencil is poised at her lips. An outside dog barks. In sleep Pedro answers a small woof. She erases the mark and writes, *A*. After a moment, she adds—*minus*.

She resets the timer.

"Again," she says.

It is dark at seven A.M. on Christmas Eve but the sun, having no options, is returning to the city. It's asking the wrought-iron fire escapes, the hydrants—*What'd I miss?* It's occurring like a memory to the buildings of the financial district. It's lighting half of Mrs. Santiago as she rises— Mrs. Santiago waxing. She points out a tugboat in the river, dew-colored jalousies. She can see the rooftop murals only the El riders can see.

IF YOU WERE HERE I'D BE HOME NOW.

Can she imagine a better morning? Would she change any part of it, even if she could? She tells the birds, the cat, the love letter, the stubborn sliver of moon that she cannot, she would not. A voice that seems to swell from the earth's core delivers the happy news—her husband is dead but she is alive! Like the pale ashes that curl and launch from the barrel fires on Ninth Street, she is fettered by nothing.

A crosswind retracts her and another voice intrudes: *Who are you to dream beyond the skyline, Mrs. Santiago? You're no better than anyone else. Go back to work, Mrs. Santiago. Freeze the fish, make the sausage, scrape scum off the plates. Freeze the work, make the work, scrape work off the work.*

This is the voice of the city. This is your tireless doubt. The rope that tethers you to the hydrant. Your half permission. Your limiting, maddening jawn. This voice comes from the Northwest pocket, the Roxborough, of your soul.

Mrs. Santiago swims to make up ground and flaps higher. Above the mural, exulting out of the brick. Above the dead rooftop gardens, trowels paused in dirt. Beyond the indescribable alloy the fire escapes make with the sun. Mrs. Santiago soars. Above the hard-backed stadiums, scowling in the dawn. Toward the slivered moon and loitering stars, now fading. Beyond the sill of William Penn.

Not today, Philadelphia. Bring your sorry shit back tomorrow.

Acknowledgments

I ask the forgiveness of the following people for, after they've given me so much, borrowing their names: Mrs. Michele Hofner (née Altimari), my sixth-grade teacher; Dr. Vincent Sherry, my college mentor; and in memory of Alexandra (Alex) Rubenstein; Mrs. Margueritte McGlynn, my high-school English teacher; and the incomparable Sandra Purcell.

These people are, literally and figuratively, The Cat's Pajamas: my relentlessly elegant agent, Claudia Ballard, and her fortuitously turned ankle; Laura Bonner; Julie Chang; everyone at William Morris; Alexis Washam, my wise, dreammaking editor; Rachel Rokicki, Sarah Bedingfield, and the kind, tireless team at Crown Publishers, who made such a special book.

Many years ago I moved to a new city and found a writer's group. Years passed as in cramped apartments with snacks we shaped ourselves into adults. To the Brooklyn Blackout Writers Group—Tim DeLizza, Aisha Gayle, Jesse Hassenger, Yuka Igarashi, Jennifer Leamy, and Alea Mitchell, thank you for being my first friends in New York.

A bouquet of sharpened Dixon Ticonderogas to: Brooklyn College's MFA program, especially

Joshua Henkin, Lou Asekoff, Michael Cunningham, and Ellen Tremper; the Center for Fiction; Hedge-brook Writer's Residency; David Horne; The Imitative Fallacies Writer's Group, members active and inactive; Adam Brown, Elizabeth L. Harris, Elliott Holt, Amelia Kahaney, Helen Phillips, and Mohan Sikka; University of Iowa Press, Scott Lindenbaum, Chris and Mary Austin Marker; *One Story*, especially Maribeth Bacha, Adina Talve-Goodman, Chris Gregory, Michael Pollock, Hannah Tinti, Karen Seligman, and Julia Strayer; Emily Rosenthal, Phyllis Trout and Brian Brooks; and Ken L. Walker.

These people have supported me since I was a lowercase *m*: Cindy Augustine, Dana, Nana, Eileen, and Ron Bertotti (thank you for the rides); Karen, Linda, and John Buleza; Tim Carr, Nicole Cavaliere, Diana Waters Davis, Brendan Gaul, Charles Hagarty, Craig Johnson, PJ and Jenna Franceski Linke, Ginger and Charlie McHugh, Scott Wein, and Sadie Ray; with special thanks to Ben Cohen, Laura Halasa, Beth Vasil, and Maryrose Roberts, who never sees why not.

The following man is the bee's knees: Jim Shepard.

The following musicians helped compose the tune of this book and in the process wove themselves into its melody: Rocco DeCicco, Brian Floody, Lester Grant, Brian Merrill, Aurelio

Pacilli, Chris Pistorino, Jason Rabinowitz, Denise Sandole, and my fellow unicorn Shawn Aileen Clark.

I'd like to symbolically adopt a star for the following people: Tsering Wangmo Dhompa, Tyler Flynn Dorholt, David Ellis, Cristina Moracho, Anne Ray, Tanya Rey (thank you for the "salsa lessons"), and my first and last reader, Tom Grattan.

To the Bertino family, to Tommy, Marianne, and Leah Dodson, my students, the editors who took a chance on me, and the lovely folks who shared their stories with me after reading mine in *Safe as Houses*: If you feel like you're a part of this, you are.

To Sophie, Scat, Fantastic Mr. Fox, and the 215, whose mark on me is so indelible a tattoo would be redundant.

Finally, to Thomas Everett Dodson, best dressed, best man, who as a little boy wore his Superman costume underneath his clothes "in case anyone needed rescuing." You say you don't wear it anymore, Ted, yet every day I see it.

Center Point Large Print
600 Brooks Road / PO Box 1
Thorndike, ME 04986-0001 USA

(207) 568-3717

US & Canada:
1 800 929-9108
www.centerpointlargeprint.com